FALL FIRESIDE

Quinn Valley Ranch, Book 5

LIZ ISAACSON

ISBN-13: 978-1638761273

CHAPTER ONE

*C*amille Quinn entered her sister's bedroom, her frustration reaching an all-time high. "Jess," she said, looking around, but her sister wasn't there.

She was probably out at Flynn's ranch, where she'd been spending more time lately. Cami flopped onto her bed, her tears not far behind. She sniffled, because she hated crying, and she wasn't going to let herself get out of control.

Not again.

Not over yet another cowboy.

Whistling met her ears before Jessie entered the room, and Cami glanced up. The whistling stopped, and Jessie said, "Oh, no. What happened?" She swooped to Cami's side, the way she always did.

"Gideon said he didn't want to go out with me again." Cami leaned into her sister's shoulder. "I just don't know what's wrong with me."

"Nothing's wrong with you," Jessie said.

"Why does this keep happening?" she asked.

"I don't know, Cami. You're cute. You're smart. You're funny. Maybe all these guys are just...losers." Jessie stroked

Cami's hair. "Granny just texted me. It was pretty unclear, because you know Granny and technology." Jessie chuckled, and Cami actually did too.

"But she has that peach delight we love, and I told her we'd come down since everyone else is off at the fair." Jessie stroked her hair back. "You want to? I mean, I know it's not a hot date on the Ferris wheel, but Granny and Gramps are pretty fun." She nudged Cami, who nodded.

"Yeah, all right." She got up and ran her hands through her hair. She normally didn't mind her natural curls, more brown than red, though the sun highlighted those auburn streaks. "Let me change first. I'm tired of wearing this belt."

"All right."

Cami could feel her sister's eyes on her as she rounded the corner and went further down the hall to the next bedroom, which was hers. She was much messier than Jessie, but she didn't care. And she didn't change right away either. In the past month or so, she'd been eating more potato chips—her favorite food—than normal, and maybe the belt was uncomfortable because she'd gained ten pounds.

Pushing the thought away, she changed quickly and ran upstairs to find Jessie chatting with someone on the phone, a smile filling her whole face. So she was talking to Flynn.

Cami paused and watched her sister, waiting for the jealousy to come. It didn't. Jessie had always been the sister on the sidelines while Cami went on date after date. Suddenly, she knew what that was like for Jessie, and regret filled her.

She entered the kitchen, and Jessie caught sight of her. She finished her call abruptly, and Cami hugged her. "Thank you for being the best sister ever."

"Oh, okay," Jessie said. She stepped back and held onto Cami's shoulders. "Why don't you go out with Clay? I know he asked you out, and you never went."

Cami didn't want to say why she'd told Clay that sure,

she'd love to go out, but then hadn't followed up with him. Harvest season had arrived, and Clay had been horribly busy, so he hadn't followed up either.

So she said, "I don't know," and hoped Jessie would let her leave it at that. She had a doubtful look in her eye, but she didn't say anything more. If there was someone who could text Clay and ask him what the heck he'd been thinking, it would be Jess. But Cami trusted her sister not to do that.

She worked on the family ranch too. She knew where to find Clay if she wanted to set up a date with him. She did... and she didn't. Her feelings were so very complicated right now, and she remained silent as she and her sister loaded up in Jessie's blue and white truck.

Jessie drove down the lane to Granny's, where they found Gramps sitting in a rocking chair on the front porch. "Gertie," he called as they got out of the truck. Cami's spirit lifted as she went up the steps to embrace her grandfather.

"Come see the turquoise eggs," he said, hugging the two girls at the same time. Gramps had just gotten several Ameraucanas, and he loved them more than anything at the moment.

"Oh, they don't have time to see your eggs," Granny said, coming out on the porch too. "Besides, I just got the peach delight out, and that's why they came." She kissed Jessie's cheek and then Cami's.

"I'll come see the eggs after we eat, Gramps, okay?" Cami said. She loved her grandparents, and she was glad she could see them often. Gramps loved ice cream more than any human alive, and when Cami needed a pick-me-up, all she had to do was get a carton out of the freezer and come down the road to the rocking chair on the front porch.

"Do we have ice cream to go with the peach delight?" Gramps asked, following the girls inside.

"Would it be peach delight without ice cream?" Granny

asked. Cami grinned and opened the drawer beside the fridge to get out the silverware. Jessie got down bowls, and Granny served the dessert.

Everyone moved over to the dining room table, where Granny had set out an old milk can filled with red, orange, and yellow flowers.

"All the fall colors," Cami said, beaming at Granny. Coming here had been exactly what her fragile heart needed. She'd never minded being the youngest, and she'd always known she'd be the last to find a fiancé and get married. Even though Jessie thought she'd be, Cami had always known she would be—and now she was.

"I'm thinking about getting new curtains," Granny said.

"Did you make these?" Cami asked.

"Yes, but they're having a bazaar at the church this weekend, and I'm thinking I'll get some there."

Cami met Jessie's eye, and they looked quickly away from one another. Cami smothered the giggles threatening to escape. She'd been set up by Granny loads of times before, and it seemed her grandmother's magic simply didn't work on Cami.

"There's that fireside series starting too," Gramps said.

"I'm not going to that," Cami said immediately.

"Why not, dear? It's a good series." Granny looked at her innocently. "We can go to the bazaar together, and then the first one on Saturday."

"Yeah," Jessie said, clearly enjoying herself. "I'm sure it'll be good."

"Are you going to go?" Cami asked, her eyebrows lifted high.

"Oh, I have plans with Flynn on Saturday night." Jessie beamed at Cami. "But you used to go to the fall firesides, every one of them."

"Yeah." Cami didn't want to explain that she'd first gone

because she was broken-hearted because of yet another disastrous relationship, and then to find a new date. Neither of those seemed like good reasons to attend a religious service, and she didn't want to admit them out loud.

"It'll be fun," Granny said. "And maybe you'll meet a man there."

"No thanks, Granny," Cami said. "I think I'm going to do what Flynn did. Thirty days. No dates. Male-fast."

Jessie made a strangled sound and shook her head. "Not a good idea, Cami."

"Why not?" She looked at her sister. "It's not like I have to follow it, but maybe I don't need to say yes to the very next person who asks me out."

"I really think you should try Clay," Jessie said.

Cami did like Clay, and she had been excited when he'd asked her out. But he must not have been as excited to go out with her, because it still hadn't happened.

"I'm texting him right now," Jessie said.

"You do that, and I will never speak to you again," Cami said.

"She's going to try her luck at the fireside," Granny said, and Cami watched as Jessie lowered her phone, a worried edge in her eye. Her sister had always looked out for her, and Cami glanced at Granny.

"Fine, Granny. I'll try my luck at the fireside." But she wasn't going to accept a date. Oh, no, she was not.

Granny's seventh attempt to set her up would fail again. But maybe the reverend would say something to soothe her ragged soul.

CAMI SMOOTHED DOWN THE MAXI DRESS, AS IT HID THE extra pounds she'd been packing on lately. She'd gone through her room and thrown out the bags of potato chips, and she'd been taking the stairs two or three times before breakfast to get in some extra steps.

It had only been three days since the peach delight with her grandparents, so it wasn't like she'd gotten rid of the weight she'd put on. Plus, she'd forgotten to look at the turquoise eggs that night, so she'd gone back last night with the banana ice cream her mother made and her excitement for colored chicken eggs at an all-time high.

The homestead felt so big these days, though her sisters all still lived here. But it wasn't the place it had used to be, full of chatter and laughter and weekend movies with flavored popcorn and too much soda.

Now, Betsy, Georgia, and Jessie spent weekends with their significant others, and for all three of them, that meant a fiancé. In fact, by April of next year—just seven months from now—all four of Cami's siblings would be married.

Maybe Granny *was* magical, as she'd been claiming responsibility for the success of her grandchildren's happiness, and not just in Cami's branch of the Quinn family. Cousins everywhere from the pub to the spa to the veterinary office had found love.

Cami sighed. She wasn't sure she wanted to start another relationship. Everything was new and exciting at first, but she worried she was shiny on the outside and completely dull on the inside. Once the men she'd gone out with rubbed off the gold, they were bored with her. Broke up with her. Or simply didn't call her back.

Or asked her out and then never set anything up.

She pushed the thoughts of Clay out of her mind. She had his number too. She could've texted him easily. In fact, she could've asked him what he was doing that night. Now that the harvest was over, maybe he'd have time to go to the fall fireside with her.

A faint horn sounded, and she gathered her skirts and hurried upstairs. Granny and Gramps sat in the truck, side-by-side, and Cami grinned at them as she skipped down the steps.

"Heya," she said.

"Are you ready for this?" Granny asked, a very proper hat on her head.

"So ready," Cami said, buckling her seatbelt.

"I think you'll meet someone tonight," Granny said. "I have a very good feeling about it."

"Okay, Granny." Cami laughed, and after a bumpy ride to the church, she climbed down and helped Granny out of the truck. They went into the church, the September evening air definitely holding a crispness to it that made Cami relax even further.

Autumn was her favorite season, and soon the leaves would be changing. Maybe when they came out of the fireside, fireflies would be buzzing in the air. Cami loved fireflies, but they didn't come to Idaho often.

"Did we get the time wrong?" Granny asked when they walked in. When she heard the choir singing, alarm pulled through Cami too. She went ahead of her grandparents to find that yes, the fireside was obviously already in progress.

And the chapel was very full.

Cowboy hats stretched from left to right, and Cami wondered if they'd be able to find a seat.

Her phone buzzed, and she lifted it up to see a message from Clay. Her heart skipped a beat, and she experienced a moment of believing she'd abandon her elderly grandparents here in favor of going out with him.

But he'd said, *There's space by me if you need a seat.*

She looked up to find one face turned back to her, an expectant smile on his face. "Over there, Granny," she whispered, pointing toward Clay.

As if they could miss him. The man stood up, and Cami was once again reminded of how handsome he was, how broad those shoulders were, how kind that smile as he ushered her grandparents onto the bench.

He looked at her, and Cami walked toward him, a grateful smile on her face. Or maybe it was a flirtatious smile. She wasn't sure.

What she was sure of was that she shouldn't have worn these heels, as one stuck on the long skirt of her maxi dress and she stumbled.

"Whoa," Clay said right out loud as he grabbed onto her. Cami felt the weight of dozens of eyes as Clay's strong arms kept her from falling all the way down.

A squeak came from her mouth as her fingers scrambled to find something to hold onto—and they found Clay's biceps.

Wow, he was strong.

Her mind blanked as she looked up into his dreamy eyes. "I got you," he said.

In the next moment, her face heated, and she struggled to get her balance back. She smoothed her hands down his arms and then up into her hair. "I'm okay."

Clay stepped out of the way so she could sit next to Granny, and Clay sat down beside Cami. There was not enough room for all of them, and she shifted closer to Granny while Clay lifted his arm around the back of the pew.

Warmth filled Cami, and a shiver ran across her shoulders from the nearness of him. So much for her swearing-off-men thing.

"Hey," he whispered, the heat from his body filling her and making her face flush. "You look great."

"Thank you," she whispered back, fighting the urge to lean into him as if she was his girlfriend. In the end, she gave up and let herself lean against him.

"Sorry we haven't been able to get together," he whispered. "Maybe I can make you lunch tomorrow after church?"

Cami turned toward him, and their faces were dangerously close. Close enough she could see the flecks of green in his blue eyes. Close enough to kiss him if she wanted to.

And oh, she wanted to.

You weren't going to say yes to the next man who asked you out, she told herself.

But she found herself saying, "Yeah, lunch would be great," before she faced the front and tried to focus on the pastor as he stood at the microphone and started his sermon. After all, it wasn't really a date if he was making lunch at his cabin. Was it?

"Great," Clay said. "We can sit together at church too, if you want. You drive with your sisters, right?"

She nodded, and Clay let his arm drop slightly so it was resting around her shoulders—just like a boyfriend would do.

And Cami didn't mind one little bit, even when Granny leaned over and whispered, "Isn't this an *amazing* fireside?"

CHAPTER TWO

Clay Martin's nerves buzzed like someone had hooked him up to a live wire. And to think he hadn't wanted to come to the Saturday evening fireside. He still couldn't believe he was there. Not only that, but that Cami Quinn sat beside him.

And really, it was more like she was nestled in his lap. He wasn't sure if he'd simply sensed her presence or if the Lord Himself had told Clay to turn around. But he had, and when he'd seen Cami, he'd typed out a text so quickly that he surely would've broken Guinness World Records.

The moment he'd asked her to lunch at his cabin, he wanted to kick himself. She'd say no to that, he knew. The Quinn family ate lunch together at the homestead every Sunday.

But she'd said yes.

Clay didn't listen to the pastor, though the opening choir number had been beautiful and rousing. Instead, his mind ran through what groceries he had in his fridge—not much—and what he could make that would impress Cami. Again, not much.

She certainly wasn't the type of woman who would appreciate grilled cheese sandwiches and canned tomato soup. He glanced at her. Was she?

Betsy was the chef in the family, and Clay couldn't remember if Cami liked cooking or not. He'd been working at Quinn Valley Ranch for six years, sure. But Cami had been off at college when he'd arrived. She'd earned her Master's degree in accounting, and come back to the ranch to run the financial side of things. She'd only been back for three years, and Clay may or may not have had his eye on the boss's daughter since then.

She went out with plenty of men, most of them cowboys like him. Nothing ever seemed to stick though, and he wondered why. Was it her? The other men? Would he stick?

Perhaps that was why he hadn't done more than ask her out. Of course, it had been harvest season, and that had required all of Clay's time—and more. Especially because Flynn Hollister had left the ranch to start his own, leaving Quinn Valley a little shorthanded.

Clay's mood soured at the thought of Flynn being gone. He wasn't sure why his friend's departure had affected him so strongly, only that it had. He didn't like people leaving, and he'd gotten very comfortable with the cowboys at Quinn Valley Ranch.

On the east side, away from the homestead and the main road onto the property, a row of four cabins stood. Clay lived by himself, in a cabin shaded by huge trees. Newt and Wyatt lived next door. Flynn could've lived in one of the cabins, but he'd opted out of the room and board part of the pay scale at the ranch.

Steven and Taylor lived in the cabin beside Newt and Wyatt, and the last cabin on the opposite end from Clay was filled with Gil and Monson. Only Clay lived alone, and he didn't entirely hate it.

He'd been doing everything alone in his life. With his next older sibling thirteen years older than him, he'd grown up as an only child. Essentially. His father had died when he was fourteen, and his mother had passed when he was twenty-five. He'd come to Idaho then, unable to stay in the state of Wyoming without any reason to do so.

His brothers weren't that interested in him, as they had their own lives, their own families, and their own ranches to deal with.

Clay pushed the thoughts away. He hated dwelling on the first twenty-five years of his life. Sure, he had had some happy memories, but the negative ones always seemed to outweigh the positive.

The congregation stood to sing, and Clay scrambled to his feet, trying to figure out which song they were singing. Cami held the book in front of her, moving it over so it was between them. He took the right side of it, wishing he could curl his fingers around hers.

Maybe.

Clay was extraordinarily bad with women, and that had probably contributed to him asking Cami for a date and then never setting anything up. He hadn't been out with anyone in a few years now, and sometimes he wondered if he even had his whole heart to give. Or if he even knew how to love someone else.

Loneliness etched its way through him, scratching his heart. His pulse picked up as the song finished.

As they sat back down, more room was made, and Cami didn't have to lean quite so far into him. A pang of regret hit him, because it sure had been nice to have that human touch. She looked at him, a smile quickly brightening her face.

Clay returned it, a silent prayer now streaming through his mind that he would know what to do when it came to Cami Quinn.

Please, Lord, he thought. *It would be nice to have a female in my life again.*

CLAY WOKE THE NEXT MORNING WITH THE SUN, AS USUAL. He didn't work every Sabbath Day, but someone had to do the basic chores. The five full-time cowboys on the ranch took turns, and along with Rhodes, that meant they only had to work one out of every three Sundays.

Today was one of Clay's, and he found Newt out on his front porch when he went outside. "Mornin," he called to the cabin one over.

"Yep," Newt said, so not a morning person. Clay smiled as he trucked down his front steps. He didn't understand a cowboy who didn't like getting up before dawn, but Newt seemed to make things work nonetheless.

"Small animals or big?" he asked as he climbed Newt's steps. The man handed him a cup of coffee, their Sabbath Day routine.

"I'll take the big ones today," Newt said.

Clay nodded, because he didn't care if he fed chickens or horses. Sometimes he'd talk to the horses, and that was nice, but he could share his secrets with the cluckers too. They didn't spread gossip, though they did squabble a lot.

The air held the hint of pine in it today, and Clay thought it would be jacket weather before long.

"How was the fireside?" Newt asked, and Clay almost slopped his coffee over the back of his hand.

"Great," he managed to say. "How was your date with Jo?"

"Great," he said, but his voice sounded hollow and flat.

"Really?"

"I hate the carnival," he said. "Fair. Whatever. It's all too noisy and too many people." Newt shook his head. "But Jo's nice. I'll probably go out with her again." Newt had met the woman online, and she lived in Lewiston, about an hour away from Quinn Valley.

"Hmm," Clay said, already thinking about his "date" with Cami that afternoon. He'd stopped at the grocery store after the fireside last night, and he felt confident he could put together something edible.

"All right." Newt groaned as he stood up. "Let's get this done so I can go back to bed."

Clay chuckled as he set his coffee mug next to Newt's on the porch railing. They loaded into the side-by-side parked between their cabins and Newt drove them over to the barns. He'd feed and water the horses and cows, putting the ones out to pasture that needed it. Clay would take care of the barn cats, the goats, the chickens, the pigs, and move over to the bulls.

They'd meet there and make sure everyone was fed and everything was done before calling their morning chores complete. Clay would text Rhodes, and he'd hurry home to shower before church.

Church.

With Cami.

That was a little forward, he knew. The Quinn sisters didn't seem to sit with their boyfriends until they were wearing diamonds, and Clay's throat turned dry at the very thought of having a relationship so serious that there might be jewelry involved.

He moved through the chores, sprinkling the feed and filling water troughs. Sweat beaded beneath his hat, and while it was September, the sun was still out in full force. By the time he made it to the bullpens, his fingers ached, and he regretted not taking any painkiller before leaving his cabin.

His mother had had severe arthritis, and Clay had inherited that from her. Too many small motor movements made his wrists and fingers hurt, but he knew how to take care of himself. He just had to do it.

His phone buzzed in his back pocket, and he pulled it out to check it. He expected to see Rhodes's name on the screen, but it was his sister's.

Cami.

Clay's breath caught in his throat, and he swiped the message open to read the whole thing. *Hey, sorry, but we always eat lunch as a family after church, and I feel weird saying I'm going to your place.*

"She's cancelling," he whispered to himself. He looked up and toward the homestead, as if Cami would be standing on the front porch, texting him. Rejecting him.

He looked back at the text. What was he supposed to say? Before he could think of anything, another one came in.

Maybe we can have lunch another day?

Sure, he typed out. *Another day is fine.*

You tell me when works for you, she said. *I'm at the homestead literally all the time.*

Clay's heartbeat crashed around in his chest. Would he be too forward if he asked her to lunch tomorrow? He got a lunch break, and she could easily get to his cabin. No one else would have to know.

Though why it would be a secret, he wasn't sure about either.

"You haven't started yet?" Newt's voice made Clay jump.

Confused, and still with chores to do, he shoved his phone in his back pocket without replying to Cami. "Just starting now," he said.

"Who were you texting?" Newt asked.

"No one," Clay said, though Cami was definitely someone.

"Well, when you text Rhodes, tell him Chocolate Shadow is acting up again. Thrown his shoes during the night and kicking the wall."

Clay sighed. "That horse."

"Yeah, well, Rhodes can come sleep with him to make sure he doesn't panic in the night," Newt said darkly. "I told him that horse was trouble." He pulled the hose over to the trough and began filling it.

Clay laughed, because Newt really was a mystery to him. He was a cowboy who hated getting up early and didn't seem to like horses. Clay shook his head and went to help feed the bulls. At least his thoughts were on something besides Cami now, though he couldn't help hoping that they might still be able to sit together at church.

A fool's hope, he told himself. If she'd cancelled lunch because she didn't want to tell her family, she wasn't going to drag all of her sisters over to his side of the chapel to sit by him.

Nope, that so wasn't going to happen.

CHAPTER THREE

*C*ami stared at her phone, willing Clay to invite her to lunch tomorrow. Or Tuesday. Or Wednesday. Any day besides Sunday would've worked—and she would've said yes.

Her phone stayed stubbornly silent.

She didn't want to attend another religious event. There was another fireside that night, one tomorrow night, and one on Wednesday. Cami had participated and enjoyed the fall fireside series in the past, but this year she felt stuck.

Disappointment cut through her, and she got in the shower so she'd have something to focus on besides Clay's refusal to set up another date. But she couldn't remember if she'd washed her hair or not, so she washed it again. By the time she went upstairs, she wasn't even sure she had two of the same shoe on.

"Morning," Betsy chirped with a smile. "There's oatmeal on the stove. You're running a bit late, aren't you?"

"Am I?" Cami never ran late. She never missed meetings or deadlines. Numbers and schedules had always appealed to her, and they made sense, always aligning perfectly. She glanced at the clock and saw that yes, she was running late. The sisters would leave for church in fifteen minutes, and she hadn't eaten or done her makeup. Or had she?

She reached up and touched her face, and no, she didn't feel any powder. So no makeup. And she had a choice to make. Food or beauty.

"Be right back," she said, dashing for the stairs again. It was a thirty-minute drive to church. She could grab a granola bar on the way out the door, but she hated doing her eyeliner on the bumpy roads that led to town.

So she brushed and swished, glossed and glistened, until she could look at Clay with a fresh face. Maybe she'd be brave enough to ask him why he hadn't suggested tomorrow for their lunch date. And if she was feeling really courageous, she'd ask him if he really wanted to go out with her. In her experience, the men who truly wanted to see her, called. They texted. They asked her what she was most interested in and what she liked to eat and when they could come pick her up.

When, not if.

Clay didn't do any of those things, and Cami's frustration with the handsome cowboy reached an all-time high. "Maybe he's not really interested," she said to her reflection. Or maybe he was at first, but her allure had worn off—just like always. Just like with every other man she'd been out with in the past year. Maybe two years.

"Cami, we're leaving," Jess called from upstairs, and Cami took one last look at herself in the mirror.

"Be brave," she whispered, and then she hurried up the steps and into the kitchen. She grabbed a breakfast bar from the pantry and ran out the back door. She hated being the last one into the truck, because then she had to climb in the backseat in a skirt and heels.

"You look cute today," Georgia said from behind the wheel.

"Thanks," Cami said, though she wasn't going for cute. She was going for pretty. Beautiful. Gorgeous. Cute was for eleven-year-olds, and Cami was twenty-seven-years-old, for crying out loud.

She munched through her fruit and grain bar on the way to church, listening to Betsy's stories about Knox's work on other farms and ranches. Jess had tons of good stories about Flynn and his new ranch too, and Cami liked gabbing with her sisters.

They made it to church, and they all piled out of the truck, still talking a mile a minute. She trailed behind when she saw Clay's truck parked in the row over from her—and he was still sitting behind the wheel. Part of her wanted to march over there and knock on the window. The other part wanted to duck her head, tuck her hair, and accept her losses.

"Jess," she said, and her sister turned toward her.

"Yeah?"

"I need some help." She glanced at Betsy and Georgia, both of whom had heard her.

"Help with what?" Georgia asked.

"It's a guy thing," she said, not wanting to make a scene. "Clay asked me to lunch today, but we always eat as a family, so I said I couldn't. Then I said another day could work, and he didn't respond."

"He's so clueless sometimes," Jess said.

"He asked me out weeks ago," Cami said, lowering her voice as a family passed them. "And never set anything up. He's probably not interested, right?"

"He's interested," Jess said. "He's just...shy."

"Shy?" Cami shook her head. "He's sitting in his truck right over there. Let's take a vote. Raise your hand if you think I should go talk to him right now and find out if he really wants to go out with me."

All three of her sister's hands went up. She groaned. "I was hoping you'd vote no to that."

Jessie smiled at her and tucked her hair behind her ear. "You go over there, and you ask him to lunch tomorrow. If he says yes, he's interested."

"What if he's busy?" Georgia asked. "That's not an indicator of his interest."

"What is, then?" Cami asked.

"I heard he had his arm around you at the fireside last night," Betsy said with a glint in her eye.

Alarm pulled through Cami. "What? Where did you hear that?"

"Oh, I took some cookies to Granny last night, after you guys got home."

"It was nothing," Cami said, not liking the way her sisters were looking at her. "Seriously. We were packed on that bench, and it was the only way to fit." It had felt nice with his arm around her though.

"We voted," Georgia said. "Go." She nudged Cami toward Clay's truck, but the bells started ringing.

"We'll be late," Cami said. "I'll talk to him after the service." She cast one last look behind her, toward Clay's truck, and saw him slide out of the front seat, his phone at his ear. He was too far away for her to hear what he was saying, and she turned away from him quickly so he wouldn't catch her staring at him.

After all, things between them were already awkward enough.

CAMI WANTED TO LEAVE THE CHAPEL AS SOON AS SHE'D SAT down. She'd heard people complain about being a third wheel or a fifth wheel, but she was the ninth wheel in her family, and it was as horrible as it sounded.

Her hip hurt from where she was smashed into the end of the pew, and the reverend was talking for a long time today. How he could give so many speeches was beyond Cami, but she liked numbers and figures for a reason. They didn't talk back.

Finally, the sermon ended, and people began filing out of the chapel. Cami stood up, ready to escape. Her bravery had failed; she would not be talking to Clay today.

"Cami," her brother said before she'd even taken a step.

"Yeah?"

"I need to talk to you about something."

She waited for her sisters to go ahead, and Rhodes asked, "Can you drive home with me?"

She glanced at his fiancée, Capri. "Sure." She smiled at her soon-to-be sister-in-law. "Is it bad?"

"No, just a little project Rhodes has in mind." Capri smiled at Cami. "He needs to know the cost and if it would be good for the ranch."

"If what would be good for the ranch?" Cami asked, looking between Rhodes and Capri. Almost everyone had left the chapel now, including Clay. So Cami didn't have to admit her lack of courage. He'd simply left before she'd had the chance to grab him.

Which was Rhodes's fault, really.

"I want to update and upgrade the irrigation system," Rhodes said.

Cami blinked. "Oh, wow."

"Yeah." Rhodes grinned at her. "Let's talk about it on the way back to the homestead. I'm starving."

"Betsy is going to pick up Knox," Cami said. "We don't have to hurry."

"Yes, we do," Rhodes said. "Because then I can stop at my

cabin and grab a snack before Betsy gets back." He grinned at Cami and started up the aisle to the exit. He didn't say anything else about this irrigation system he had in mind until the three of them were seated in the cab of his truck.

"I want a cost analysis," he said. "I want the well updated, and I need copies of all of our water rights." He continued on, talking about sprinklers and systems and what he envisioned for the ranch.

Cami loved her older brother, and his drive for improving the ranch. His enthusiasm for the future was admirable, but a keen sense of being overwhelmed made her hold up her hand. "Rhodes, slow down," she said. "You have plans for all of this?"

"I've been working on it for a month or so," he said. "Flynn has a great system out at his place, and Quinn Valley is in dire need of an upgrade." He glanced at Cami. "I need to know how much it's going to cost and if we can afford it."

"I'm not as familiar with the ranch as you are," Cami said. "You'll have to show me around, talk me through some things. Then I can do all the numbers, but my guess is we'll be able to implement what you want."

"Yeah?" Rhodes looked and sounded so hopeful.

"Yeah," Cami said. "Leo was really great with the ranch finances." In fact, all Cami was trying to do was keep up that tradition. Not kill the systems their last accountant had put in place. She'd spent a lot of the last three years talking to her mom and dad about the money, as they'd taken over for eight months in between the time Cami graduated and when Leo had retired.

"Great," Rhodes said, turning onto the road that led to the ranch. "I'm going to assign the project to Clay. He'll show you around, walk you through everything."

Cami sucked in a breath, her chest suddenly so tight. "No," she managed to say.

"No, what?" Rhodes asked. "Clay's the second, Cami. He knows everything I know."

"I...." Cami didn't know what to say.

Rhodes pulled into his driveway and put the truck in park, looking past Capri to Cami. "I haven't talked to him yet," he said. "But he'll be stoked. He loves doing new projects."

Did he? Cami didn't know that, and annoyance pounced through her that she didn't.

Capri put her hand on Rhodes's forearm. "Sweetheart."

"What?" He looked at her, pure confusion in his expression.

"Go get your snack," Cami said before Capri could rat her out for having a huge crush on Clay. She wasn't even sure she had a crush. He dominated her thoughts, sure, but not in a good way. Not really.

She just needed to know how he felt about her. Period. Then she'd be able to make a decision, move forward. Stop second-guessing if she'd washed her hair, and then wash it again. Stop obsessing about talking to him or not talking to him.

Rhodes said, "I'm missing something," and got out of the truck.

"How could he not know?" Capri asked.

"Know what?" Cami asked.

"About you and Clay."

"There is no me and Clay."

"Clay probably talks more to Jessie about his crush on you than Rhodes," Capri mused as if Cami hadn't spoken. And she was totally right. Clay and Jess were pretty good friends, something Cami had never minded. But now, she envied their friendship and how much Jess knew about Clay.

Cami really needed to stop thinking about him. Curse Granny and her magical matchmaking skills. Without all of that, she would've just thought Clay a nice guy for having a few seats at the fireside.

No, Granny had nothing to do with this turmoil inside Cami. Clay had asked her out weeks ago and done nothing.

This unrest in her soul belonged to him.

Rhodes returned with a bag of white chocolate popcorn. "Ready?"

"Yes," Capri said, giving Cami a knowing look.

"So I'll talk to Clay in the morning," he said as if Cami hadn't protested. "Can you come to our agriculture meeting?" He glanced at Cami as he backed out of his driveway.

She didn't know how to tell him no. Besides, it was her job, and it made sense for Clay to head up a project like this, not only because he was second-in-command around the ranch, but because he was the lead cowboy over their crops.

"What about Joey?" Cami asked anyway.

"Joey's quitting at the end of the month," Rhodes said. "I'm going to have Gil take over anything Clay can't handle."

So she'd have to work with Clay on this project.

Fine.

She could be professional and distant, the way he'd been even after asking her out. She looked at Capri, who patted her leg with a smile, and then they arrived at the homestead, Georgia rumbling up behind them a moment later.

Betsy and Knox arrived before Cami could even get out of the truck, and she was sincerely hoping she didn't have any room in her brain to keep thinking about Clay.

She'd see him tomorrow anyway, and even that was sooner than she'd like.

CHAPTER FOUR

*C*lay made himself the sorry grilled cheese sandwiches for lunch. He skipped the tomato soup, though something hot to fill his stomach sounded good.

He sat on the couch for about four seconds before he couldn't stand to be caged by his cabin walls. "Come on," he said to his dog, a golden retriever German shepherd mix. The dog was as smart as a whip, though Clay had only owned him for ten months.

He loved to chase a ball, and he would search the long grass for it until he found it. His patience was never-ending, and Clay loved watching Trooper do what he loved to do—find and hunt and fetch.

"Let's go run," he said to the dog, picking up a couple of tennis balls and Trooper's leash. He wouldn't use the leash, because they only ran from his cabin to the stand of trees about a half a mile away. Clay wouldn't run much further than that, because he hated running, and Trooper wasn't a rabid dog trying to rip off his arms.

He opened the front door, and Trooper bolted out in front of him. His claws clicked on the steps that led to the front yard, and the dog barked once he reached the lawn. His way of saying, *Come on, human. Move faster.*

Clay took his time stretching, and then he threw a ball as far as he could down the lane. Trooper barked as he took off after it, and Clay kept the other ball in his hand as he started after the dog.

When Trooper saw him coming, he barked, which caused him to drop the ball. "Come on," Clay said, reaching the dog. "Get it, and let's go."

Trooper grabbed the ball again and ran ahead of Clay. Soon enough, their paces evened out, and Clay kept his focus on the trees in the distance. They hardly seemed to get closer, but he did eventually reach them. "All right," he said, panting almost as hard as the canine. "Drop the ball."

Trooper did what Clay said, and he threw the ball again, this time out into the field with all the grass. The dog was so vocal as he looked for the ball, and he pounced and yapped as he found the ball and trotted back to Clay with it.

The game continued, and Clay had to pay close attention to Trooper, because the dog would literally not quit on his own. After a while, Clay's throwing arm ached, and he started back toward the cabins. Trooper walked at his side, his tongue hanging out of his mouth.

Back home, Clay got water for himself and the dog, and he tried sitting on the couch again. There was just no way that was going to happen today. He thought of Cami on the other side of the ranch, with her family.

Surely lunch had ended over there by now, and he wondered what she did after that. Take a nap? Play games with her siblings? Watch a movie?

Clay sometimes did all of those things, except for spending time with his siblings. But he might go next door and play cards with the other cowboys. Jessie had promised to teach him all of her tricks, but she hadn't come to poker night again.

She probably never would, and Clay would keep trying to outwit the other men who showed up every first Thursday to the far barn for poker night.

"A shower," he said to himself. That would take at least twenty minutes, and he was sweaty from the run down the road.

Twenty minutes later, and he came face-to-face with his phone. He'd sat in his truck in the church parking lot, staring at his device too. Trying to find a way to text Cami and ask her to come to dinner tonight.

Surely her family didn't eat every meal together on the Sabbath. But Clay hadn't been able to find the right words, and Flynn had called about another mechanical issue on his ranch. Clay had talked to him until the church bells rang, and then he'd hurried inside.

He still hadn't had any more contact with Cami, and he felt like he was going insane. He swiped and tapped and got to his and Cami's text string.

What are you doing for dinner tonight?

He stared at the words, trying to decide if they were too forward. Cami didn't seem to get scared by men who came right out and said what they wanted. Clay simply didn't know how to do that.

His heart skipped over a couple of beats, and he read the words again, quickly tapping the send arrow before he could erase them.

Trooper barked from his spot on the couch, and a few moments later, someone knocked on Clay's front door. Confusion ran through him. Was it Cami? That made no sense, and sure enough, the door opened a moment later and Wyatt walked in.

"Hey," he said with a smile. "A few of us are setting up a badminton net in the back yard. You want to come play?"

"Sure," Clay said, feeling foolish for asking Cami to dinner. He might be lonely, but he had friends he could rely on. "Hey, so can I ask you a quick question first?"

"Sure." Wyatt picked up a bag of chips and ate a couple. "What's goin' on?"

"It's about...Cami Quinn."

"Oh, boy," Wyatt said with a smile, his eyes glowing with happiness now. "You asked her out ages ago. You ever gonna follow up on that?"

"I did," Clay said. "And I kind of blew it."

"How so?"

"I don't really know," Clay said. He held out his phone. "Read the texts. I asked her to lunch yesterday at the fall fireside."

Wyatt took the phone and read the texts. "Sounds like you did great to me." He handed the phone back. "And it looks like you won't be playing badminton."

"What?"

"She answered, cowboy. You didn't see her response?"

No, he hadn't, and Clay took his phone and looked at it. *I can squeeze in dinner before the fireside tonight. Should we eat and attend that together?*

"The fireside," he said. He had been planning on attending, but he'd lost sight of it in his attempts to get Cami off his mind.

"I'll tell the others you're out," Wyatt said, laughing as he left.

Clay said, "Yeah, okay," as he tapped out a response to Cami. *Yeah, sure. That sounds great. What time do you want to come by?*

Whenever you're ready, Cami said.

I'm ready now.

Great, she said. *I'll be over in a few.*

Clay's whole body felt like he'd been encased in fire, and he turned in a full circle. Trooper barked, and Clay focused on the dog. "Yeah, okay. Calm down. Yes, calm." He could do calm. He could.

"What should we have for dinner?" he asked. He wasn't terribly hungry, and he had no idea what time it was. He strode over to the fridge and yanked it open, though he already knew what groceries he had.

He glanced at the clock and decided he didn't need to start the pizza right now. It was only four, and surely Cami wouldn't come until closer to dinner time. After all, the fireside didn't start until seven-thirty. They didn't need to "squeeze in" dinner.

He glanced around his house, realizing it wasn't the cleanest on the planet. He started straightening up, putting his dirty dishes in the sink, along with the frying pan he'd used to make his lunch. He opened a cupboard and put away his salt and pepper shakers, moved his paper towels next to the fridge, and pulled out a lighter to light the candle that smelled like oranges and vanilla.

Jessie had given him the candle for his last birthday, and he wondered if she could give him some insight on her sister. *Nope*, he told himself. He wasn't going to get information on Cami from Jessie.

He wanted it from Cami.

Trooper barked and jumped off the couch, going right to the door. Clay froze. She couldn't be here already. Could she?

A light, very feminine knock sounded on the door, and Clay's pulse went crazy. He strode over to the door and opened it, revealing a beautiful Cami Quinn standing there. She wore the same dress she'd worn to church, minus the heels. Her dark red hair flowed over her shoulders in pretty curls, and Clay couldn't help smiling at her.

"Hey," he said, standing in the doorway and grinning for all he was worth. Trooper sat behind Clay's leg, as he'd been taught to do, and Clay felt like the earth was spinning way too fast.

"Hey." Cami smiled at him, her fingers twining around themselves.

"Do you like pizza?" he asked.

"Who doesn't like pizza?"

Clay chuckled and ducked his head, adjusting his cowboy hat slightly. "I hear you. Well, come in. I have stuff to make pizza, and we can each make our own."

Cami ducked past him, gathering her long skirt in one hand and tucking her hair with the other. "Can I pet your dog?"

"Of course," Clay said, bringing the door closed behind her. He could not believe this was happening. Cami was in his house. *His* house. "His name is Trooper."

"He's adorable." She crouched down in front of Trooper and started scratching behind his ears. "And so soft." She glanced up at Clay, and something electric jumped from her gaze to his. He blinked, sure he was the only one who could feel that.

Cami straightened. "I like meats and veggies," she said. "What do you have for toppings?"

Clay hopped into action and opened the fridge again. "I have green peppers. Let's see...onions. Olives. I bet I have black olives in the cupboard." He knew he was scrambling, and he told himself to calm down. He took a deep breath, and then another one.

"How was your family lunch?"

"Oh, Betsy burned the rolls, so she was all out of sorts." Cami gave a light laugh that lit up Clay's whole soul.

"That doesn't sound like her." He'd eaten plenty of Betsy's food. As the ranch chef, she sometimes invited all the cowboys to the homestead for lunch. It was there that Clay had first met Cami and been struck with her kind spirit and gorgeous face.

"Well, we all have bad days." Cami smiled at him and opened a drawer. "Knife...knife."

"Here," he said, taking a knife from the butcher block next to the fridge.

"Tell me about your family," Cami said as she took the knife.

Clay sucked in a breath and held it. She must've noticed, because she said, "If you want. It's fine if...I noticed you never go see them at holidays or anything."

She'd noticed?

Clay set a pan on the stove and got out the sausage and ground beef. She said she liked meats on her pizza, and he did too. "Uh, let's see. I have two older brothers. Like, *way* older than me. Joe is fifty, and Jerry is forty-six."

"Oh." Pure surprise coated those two little letters.

"Yeah." Clay nodded, got the heat going under the pan, and started unwrapping the sausage so he could brown it all up. "I mean, we get along okay. It's more like we don't know each other at all. I was thirteen when Jerry got married, and my dad died the next year." He shook his head, his focus only on the pan in front of him.

His childhood and past wasn't painful. He just didn't like talking about it. Or maybe it was painful.

"I'm so sorry." Cami touched his left arm, and Clay looked at her. That heat passed between them again, but Clay told himself it was just the fire under the frying pan. Cami's face filled with a flush, and she fell back a step.

Clay cleared his throat. "Yeah," he said, though he didn't know why. "I went to college for a year, but then I got in a pretty bad mountain biking accident. I went back home, and my mom took care of me until I recovered all the way." He swallowed. Yep, this part was definitely painful. "And then she died too. So, with nothing and no one keeping me in Wyoming, I came to Idaho. I worked on any ranch or farm that needed me, and I landed here six years ago."

"When I was in college," she said.

"Right." Clay broke up the sausage and ground beef, the scent of the cooking meat starting to fill the air. "Listen, I just...." He turned around and faced her fully. "I'm sorry it took me so long to set up a date. Sometimes...." He tried to find the right words, but he'd never been particularly good with them.

"I get it," Cami said. "Sometimes we just don't know what to do or say, so we don't do or say anything."

Relief filled Clay. "Right. Are you like that too?"

She grinned and tucked that pretty hair again. "Why do you think I went into a career that deals with numbers?" She laughed, and somehow that made everything better in Clay's life. She leaned closer to him, almost like she had a secret to share. "Numbers make sense," she said. "People don't."

And boy, wasn't that the truth?

CHAPTER FIVE

$\mathcal{C}$ami had never experienced a better hour than the one making personal pizzas in Clay's kitchen. Once he'd told her the more sobering story of his family—which was short, and surely there was more to learn there—they'd settled into an easy conversation about the ranch.

His dog. The bulls. What she liked on her pizza. Their favorite sodas.

As the pizzas baked, Clay took her outside and showed her what Trooper could do. "I can't believe he'll high five," she said, holding up her hand again. "How'd you learn to teach him all of this?"

"Okay, don't laugh," Clay said, and Cami found him downright refreshing. Jess had always said he was one of the good ones, but Cami hadn't known what that meant until now. Maybe she'd spent so much time with the bad ones that now she could see it.

"But Internet videos," he said. "There's a ton of information on dog tricks on the Internet."

Cami giggled, something she wished she wouldn't do quite

so often. She thought it made her sound childish, or worse, air-headed. "I bet there is."

"Plus, Trooper's smart," Clay said. "That helps a lot."

"Have you done a lot of dog training?"

"A little, actually," he said, settling on the steps with the tennis ball. Trooper sat at the bottom of them, an expectant look on his face. "After I got hurt, I had a dog that worked with me."

"Worked with you?"

"Yeah." He threw the ball, and Trooper tore after it. "Like, a therapy dog? He went with me to the store, on my walks, that kind of stuff." Clay cut her a glance out of the corner of his eye. "I think he was more of an emotional support animal. I'd always liked dogs, but I found a new respect for them after that."

Cami sat beside him as Trooper returned with the ball. He dropped it, slobbery and covered in grass, at the bottom of the steps.

"I'm not throwin' that again," Clay said to the dog. "We already ran and played fetch today."

Cami reached for it, but Clay put his hand on her arm. "I wouldn't. He's relentless. And you don't want to touch that, trust me."

The tennis ball did look disgusting, and Cami sat back down. Clay reached over and slid his hand into hers. "Is this okay?" he whispered, almost like he was afraid she'd disappear into thin air if he spoke too loud.

Shooting fireworks moved through Cami's fingers, up her arm, and zinged across her shoulders. "Yeah," she said just as reverently. She felt like Cinderella, like when this night ended, he'd disappear back into his castle—or his cabin—and she wouldn't see him again.

Clay Martin was more mysterious than she'd thought, but he had a gentle power about him that spoke to Cami. Made her want to get closer and learn more about him. His hand in hers was warm, and strong, and callused, and she liked that. It spoke of his work ethic and personality.

"Favorite hobby," she said, leaning her head against his shoulder.

He sighed, and it sounded so happy. "I like playing with Trooper," he said. "But I'm not sure that's a hobby. I like collecting things."

"What kind of things?"

"Uh, all kinds of things," he said. "But mostly antiques. Anything from the war eras fascinates me. Anything old that we don't use anymore that used to be so important. And Christmas stuff. Well, not just stuff. Santa Clauses and nativities." He shifted on the steps, and Cami sensed his discomfort. But he was talking to her about real things, and that was more than a lot of the other men she'd dated had done.

"What's in your collection that's old that we don't use anymore?"

"Radios," he said. "I mean, if I want to listen to music now, I use my phone and a Bluetooth speaker. But only sixty or seventy years ago, people had radios in their homes. It was how they stayed connected to the world." His voice took on a new quality as he spoke, and Cami appreciated that he had more to him than a cowboy hat and a pair of sexy boots.

She liked those things too, but it was nice to know the man had depth too.

"What else?"

"I have an old water bag I found at a flea market in Jackson Hole," he said. "They used to wet them down and fill them with water and put them on the front of their cars. That way, if the car overheated, they'd have water to put in the radiator."

Cami had never heard of such a thing. "I want to see your collection."

"Uh...." Clay started laughing. "We'll have to save that for another time. The timer's going off on our dinner." He stood up, brushed off his jeans, and extended his hand to her. She put hers right back in his and let him pull her up, though she could've stood on her own.

Their eyes met, and electricity zipped through his expression and into her body, making her cells sing. In the kitchen, he expertly removed their pizzas from the oven and set them on the stovetop, just the way Betsy did.

"Let's see," he said, turning to the fridge. "I bought a salad too." He opened a bag of salad and poured it into a bowl. Cami liked that he was somewhat proficient in the kitchen, and she simply sat at the bar and watched him. He got down plates and put forks on the counter. "Okay. We're ready." He looked at her again, and she could get lost in eyes like that. "Do you mind if I say grace?"

She folded her arms. "Not at all." She closed her eyes as he began. She wasn't entirely sure what he said, because his voice was like a river of chocolate. Warm, and melty, and oh-so-tantalizing. But when he said, "Amen," she did too, and then he served her the pizza she'd made for herself.

"All right, Miss Cami," he said, sitting beside her and pulling the bowl of salad over to them. "I've told you all kinds of stuff about me. Tell me something about you I don't know."

"I'm an open book," she said. "You already know heaps of stuff about me."

"That's not true," he said. "I barely know you at all."

"Jessie doesn't tell you things?"

A frown marred that beautiful face. "Why would Jessie and I talk about you?" He looked at her, the salad tongs poised above the bowl.

Cami shrugged, feeling a bit foolish. "I don't know."

"Tell me about your family."

"You know my family," she said.

"Sort of," he said. "What about all your cousins?"

"You must go out of your mind when we have parties here at the ranch." A light came on in her mind. "Do you?"

"It's a lot of people to handle," he admitted. "But I kind of like it. Your family shows me that not all families are like mine. That maybe I could have a family that wants me around someday."

The air went right out of Cami's lungs. "Clay. I'm—I didn't know." She also didn't know what to say to make the pinch around his eyes disappear.

He smiled, and that did it, though Cami was well-versed in smiling through the pain. "It's okay, Cami. Really." He finished putting the salad on his plate and lifted a slice of pizza to his lips.

Cami watched him take a bite, her stomach filling with fire. She couldn't seem to do more than breathe and blink, and Clay's face turned into a question.

"You aren't going to eat?" he asked.

"Oh, yes." She tore her gaze from his mouth and picked up her own pizza. "We better hurry up. The fireside starts in an hour, and we have quite the drive to get there."

CAMI STOOD WITH THE REST OF THE CROWD THAT HAD come out for the Sunday evening fireside. The night had grown chilly in the past hour, and Pastor Dahl had opted to give his message outside in the amphitheater.

She shivered, and Clay glanced at her. "Cold?"

"Yeah."

The music began just as Clay slipped his arm around her and pulled her closer to him. Cami felt the weight of every eye in the county, but when she covertly scanned the people around her, she couldn't find anyone looking at her.

So maybe she just felt a bit self-conscious standing so close to Clay, within eyeshot of so many people. She barely sang the closing hymn, though Clay sang out in a beautiful bass voice. She could listen to him sing all night long, and she stopped vocalizing near the end of the song.

Everyone sat, and Cami closed her eyes for the closing prayer. They'd barely said amen before Clay slipped his hand into her and leaned toward her. "Dessert?"

"What did you have in mind?"

"Nothing," he said. "I just suddenly wanted some ice cream."

"The best shop for that is closed on Sundays," Cami said, an idea percolating in her mind. She faced Clay, their gazes locking. "But my mother makes an amazing banana ice cream, and we have some leftovers at the homestead."

Clay's eyebrows rose. "What goes on at the homestead in the evenings?"

"Nothing." Cami giggled and pushed a palm against his chest. "You make it sound like we're doing something scandalous over there."

"It's quiet on Sundays, I know that," he said.

"Yeah, because we're all napping. Oooh, alert the authorities."

He laughed, and Cami sure did like that she'd been the one to make him do it. She stood up, keeping her hand in his. "Come on. We have homemade hot fudge and caramel sauce too, courtesy of Granny. We can have a private banana split party."

Clay came with her, and Cami felt like she was walking on clouds as they moved back to his truck. Once he'd helped her into the front seat, she hurried to pull out her phone and text Betsy.

I want the kitchen and living room for me and Clay. Doable?

Her sister didn't answer right away, and Clay got behind the wheel. "Ready?"

"Ready," she said, shoving her phone under her thigh. Now all she had to do was pray that her sisters would find somewhere else to be so she could be alone with Clay.

CHAPTER SIX

Clay walked a couple of steps behind Cami as she climbed the steps to the homestead. It was clear they would not be having a private banana split party, if the light and laughter spilling from the homestead was any indication.

He didn't mind, but Cami didn't seem too happy when she turned back when she reached the front door. "Sorry," she said. "We might have to fight for the ice cream."

"It's fine," he said. He didn't even care if there was any ice cream. Spending time with Cami was more of the treat he'd wanted.

"Are you ready for the crazy?" she asked, pressing her back into the door. "Betsy said everyone is playing charades, and let's just say my family isn't quiet." A roar from inside accompanied the last word, and Clay grinned at her.

"I know what your family is like," he said, wondering why she looked so apprehensive. "Cami, I'm fine around people."

"I know."

"Do you?" he asked. Because he didn't need her treating him like an invalid. He hated telling people about his parents, because once they knew he was an orphan, they treated him differently. The only people who hadn't were Rhodes, Flynn, and Jessie.

"Yes," Cami said.

"I play poker with people," he said. "Your sister."

"I know." She turned and opened the door, a literal wall of noise hitting Clay in the face.

Here we go, he told himself as he followed Cami inside. His breath vibrated in his chest, because everyone in the house was engaged. All four of Cami's siblings were there, with their significant others. And he was on his first date.

"Cami's here," Betsy said, coming over to greet them both. "Heya, Clay."

"Betsy. Is Jessie winning everything?"

"Surprisingly, no. I think some of Flynn's bad luck is rubbing off on her."

"I heard that," Flynn said darkly as he passed behind Betsy, his hands full of ice cream-soiled bowls. "And it's not true. We're up by six points."

Betsy rolled her eyes. "So maybe they're winning. Come on. Rhodes went to grab some more ice cream from Mom's freezer."

"Is there any of that banana left?"

"No," Jessie said, stepping over to hug Cami. Clay stood there, feeling a little out of place, though he knew these people. "Logan made short work of that. But Rhodes said he saw some strawberry the other day." She glanced at Clay. "Hey, Clay. How was the fireside?"

Jessie had always been good at including him in the conversation, and he smiled at her. "It was nice. We got to sit outside and everything."

"Granny would've been mad," Cami said. "I'm glad she didn't come."

"She said her work was done." Jessie grinned at Cami. "I'm going to go get out the graham crackers and chocolate."

Cami faded back to Clay's side, which sent a blip of happiness through him. "She dips the graham crackers in chocolate and then uses them like a spoon for the ice cream."

"Sounds amazing," Clay said.

The back door opened, and Rhodes entered with a huge bucket of ice cream. "Tons of strawberry," he said, and everyone moved into the kitchen.

Clay immediately felt uncomfortable. Maybe it was the addition of his boss. Or the way Cami tugged on his hand to get him to come with her, as if he belonged there. Nerves moved through him, and he smiled at Knox. The farrier had come to poker night a few times, and Clay had worked with him a lot with the horses.

"Hey, Clay," Rhodes said, sliding his eyes down to where Cami's hand was linked with Clay's. "How was the fireside?" He extended his hand for Clay to shake, which he did. In the next moment, Capri, Rhodes's fiancée, stepped to his side and wrapped her arms around Rhodes.

"We should've gone," she said.

"There's another one tomorrow," Rhodes said, "Right?" He looked back and forth between Cami and Clay, his eyes full of questions.

"Right," Clay said. "And it was a good message tonight. Pastor Dahl talked about not comparing your journey to anyone else's." He looked at Cami. "I really liked it." He needed a reminder sometimes that life was good—no matter what road he'd been on to get where he was.

"I didn't listen as closely as Clay, obviously," Cami said.

"I bet not," Rhodes said dryly. Clay wasn't sure what had just been said silently, but Cami giggled and swatted her brother's shoulder.

"Don't embarrass me."

"Hot fudge is ready," Betsy announced, and Clay turned toward her. She'd also chopped bananas, and Georgia opened the fridge and put a couple of cans of whipped cream on the counter. Canned whipped cream—Clay's favorite.

"I love that stuff," he told Cami, who grinned at him.

"You know you can make it, right? And it's so much better."

"Why is Betsy letting us eat that then?" Clay lifted his eyebrows, a smile touching his lips.

"We're in a pinch," Cami said.

"Yeah, I don't think so." Clay took a couple of steps over to the counter as Logan reached for a bowl. The activity of putting together an ice cream sundae started, and with ten people in the kitchen, the spirit of family and friendship blazed into the atmosphere. Clay laughed with his friends, and marveled that he could enjoy being with so many people.

The Fourth of July celebrations, Harvest feast, and other big events at the ranch usually brought out some of his worst anxiety.

But with just Cami and her siblings, along with those they loved, Clay felt...comfortable. Like he belonged.

And it was the best feeling in the world.

THE NEXT MORNING, CLAY WOKE WITH A SMILE ON HIS face. He stayed in bed while Trooper shifted, sifting through his memories from the day before.

"Cami." He sat up and swung his legs over the side of the bed. He always had a six a.m. alarm set, but it hadn't gone off yet. The morning was still quite dark, since autumn had arrived, and he stretched his arms above his head.

Stretching was something he paid close attention to, especially after his accident. He had a series of things he did each day. Stretch, self, spirit, significant others, space, safety.

At the end of the day, he evaluated the day to make sure he was taking care of himself, as well as the other things the Lord had entrusted him with.

He almost always counted animals as his significant others, but sometimes he did an act of service for another cowboy or cowgirl on the ranch. He stretched. He did something for himself every day—and he usually counted a dessert in the evening as that item. He took care of his space—doing dishes, running a load of laundry, pushing the vacuum cleaner back and forth—and he did something to feed his spirit each day.

The fall firesides had been his answer to his spirit requirement the past few days, and he couldn't wait until the sermon that evening.

Because he was once again attending with Cami. Not only that, but he'd asked her if she'd like to get dinner in town before the service. She'd ducked her head and said yes, and Clay had left her standing on the front porch.

After all, he couldn't kiss her in front of all of her siblings. He grabbed his phone, but with the early hour, she hadn't texted. He wasn't going to text her when he'd see her later, so he got in the shower, made coffee, and got over to the ranch to begin his chores.

Rhodes had Monday morning meetings with his supervisors, and Clay had overseen several parts of the ranch over the years. At the moment, he headed up the agricultural operations on the ranch, and Rhodes had asked him to start thinking about taking on a new title—foreman.

"You're the foreman," Clay has said.

"No," Rhodes said. "I'm the owner." He'd frowned when he'd said it, and no titles had been formally announced to the cowboys. But Clay was glad Rhodes trusted him enough to think he could run the whole ranch, all the cowboys, and everything.

Not that Rhodes was going anywhere. Clay knew that. He was still grateful and glad he was valuable to Quinn Valley Ranch.

He worked through the horses he was assigned to tend to that morning, and the moment he entered the homestead, he knew something was afoot.

Number one, the scent of maple syrup hung in the air, and Betsy rarely made breakfast. Number two, Cami came out of the office where Clay normally met with Rhodes. Her face burst into a grin, and she asked, "Are you ready for this?"

"Ready for what?"

"Rhodes didn't talk to you?" She approached him, easily slipping both of her hands into his.

"No." He gazed down at her, trying to pinpoint what it was about her that spoke so clearly to his soul. "What's going on?"

"He wants a completely new irrigation system." She released him and stepped over to the kitchen. "Betsy made breakfast, and there's leftovers if you want some."

"Is Rhodes here?"

"Yeah," she said, picking up a plate and putting a slice of bacon on it. Clay warred with himself. The beautiful woman —with bacon—or talking to his boss about what "a completely new irrigation system" meant.

Before he could decide, Rhodes came out of the office. "Morning," he said, no smile in sight. "Cami, is this number right?" He held a tablet and to Clay's great surprise, he held it away from his face. "I think I might need glasses."

"That's because you're an old man now," Wyatt said, coming into the kitchen from the mud room. Clay grinned at

Wyatt's comment, because watching Rhodes try to look at the screen of the tablet was pretty funny.

"It's right," Cami said.

"We can totally afford this then," Rhodes said.

"We can," she said. "Doesn't mean you can go crazy, Rhodes."

"When have I ever gone crazy?" he asked, and Clay decided waiting in the office for the meeting to start would be safer. Rhodes had just redone the landscaping at the homestead that summer, and things had gotten a little crazy.

That wasn't his fault, Clay supposed, but that of a certain bull that had gotten out and caused mayhem on the new yard. But Rhodes did like his toys, and Wyatt said, "You bought four new ATVs just last week," as Clay went into the office, baconless.

"We needed those," Rhodes said.

Cami laughed, and Clay smiled to himself. She came into the office a few seconds later and extended the plate with French toast and bacon on it to him. "Do you want to eat?"

"Not your food."

"I've eaten," she said, and he took the plate as she sat beside him.

"Thank you," he said, looking at her.

That spark came to life, and the other two cowboys talking in the kitchen muted. Cami stretched up and kissed his cheek, and then boot-steps sounded loudly in his ears as her brother entered.

Clay's whole face heated, and he kept his eyes down, the brim of his cowboy hat concealing the blush. He picked up a slice of bacon and took a bite while Cami giggled quietly beside him.

"All right," Rhodes said, a sigh leaking from his mouth. "Let's go over this project. Clay, I'm going to need you to run point on this new irrigation system, and you and Cami need to make sure we don't go over budget."

He got to work closely with Cami?

"No problem," he said, looking up and wishing his voice wasn't quite so hoarse. If Rhodes or Wyatt noticed, they didn't act like it. But Clay didn't dare look at Cami, for fear that his face would burst into flames again.

CHAPTER SEVEN

*C*ami worked at her desk in the office she shared with Rhodes. The meeting had ended hours ago, and Betsy had been busy making lunch for the whole ranch. The texts had gone out, and the cowboys should be showing up any minute.

Her stomach growled, and she couldn't wait to eat the baked potato soup Betsy had put together. The scent of freshly baked bread hung in the air, and the back door opened as the first cowboy arrived.

She refused to look up to see if it was Clay. She couldn't believe she'd kissed him that morning, only moments before her brother and Wyatt had come in. He'd reacted with a flush staining his neck and face that Cami found really cute.

She sighed, and when the sound reached her ears, she realized how much trouble she was in. Sighing all softly like that?

So she liked Clay Martin. It wasn't that big of a deal.

Don't fall too fast, she told herself. After all, she'd sighed like this with Malcolm too. And the cowboy before him. And Gideon after.

She hadn't quite made it out of the shine stage with Clay

yet, but she paused in her spreadsheet and looked out the window. "Please let him stick around after the newness of this has worn off," she prayed, her voice barely meeting her own ears.

The chatter in the house increased as more cowboys arrived, but Cami stayed at her desk. Yes, in the past, she'd made a point to go out and socialize with everyone. After all, the men who worked on the ranch were her dating pool, and she'd been out with a few of them. Nothing had ever been so serious that any awkwardness remained after the relationship ended, and that actually made Cami frown at her computer.

She heard Betsy call everyone to attention, and still, she didn't get up and go join everyone in the kitchen. For some reason, she didn't feel like talking today. Smiling at everyone. After all, she was the happy-go-lucky sister. Jessie got to glower. Betsy got to entertain. Georgia hung at the back of the crowd.

Cami was the one who went around and chatted, flirted, touched biceps, and asked how things were going. She didn't work out on the ranch in the same way as Georgia or Jessie, and she wasn't as public of a face as Betsy. She'd had to do something to get people to notice her, especially after being gone from the family ranch for so long.

Today, though, she didn't. She wasn't working, but she let her mind wander as she watched an autumn thunderstorm begin to darken the sky.

"Baked potato soup," Clay said, setting a bowl down beside her. It was garnished with cheddar cheese, green onions, and bacon, just the way she liked it.

"Oh," she said, surprise filling her. Even more shock bolted through her when he turned and closed the door, effectively drowning out some of the noise from the lunch happening in the kitchen and dining room.

He returned to her desk and pulled up a chair. "Is it okay

if we eat together?" He nodded to the bowl of soup. "Betsy said that was your favorite. She got it all set up for me." A soft, genuine, gorgeous smile adorned his face as he extended a spoon toward her.

"Thank you," she said, pure happiness and gratitude moving through her. "And this is my favorite. What kind did you get?"

"Chicken noodle," he said. "It's my favorite."

"Did your mom make it for you growing up?" she asked, realizing half a beat too late that she shouldn't have asked him that.

"No," he said. "But my dad did a couple of times when I was really sick." Something foreign and that she couldn't identify moved through his expression. "My mom wasn't very domestic."

"Oh," Cami said, trying to think of something else to say. "I don't know what I'm going to do when Betsy gets married and moves out."

"No?" Clay took a bite of noodles and carrot. "You don't cook?"

"I mean, a little bit," she said.

"I'm good at sandwiches," he said. "And hey, I'm thirty-three-years-old and haven't died of starvation yet." He kicked a grin in her direction, and Cami finally relaxed enough to dip her spoon into her soup.

"I love soup in the fall."

"It's the perfect meal," he agreed. "Do you like sandwiches?"

"Sure," she said. "What's your favorite kind?"

"Oh, I don't know," he said, but his voice pitched up a couple of notes.

"Come on," she said, teasing him. "You can tell me."

"It won't sound good."

"Then you'll have to make it for me."

Clay chuckled and shook his head. "I don't know about that. It's something we always took when we'd go hiking. In fact, I never make it if I'm not planning on loading up a backpack and hiking up to a waterfall or something."

"Not many waterfalls here," she said. "Springs, I guess."

"Sure, a spring works," he said.

"So we'll hike to a spring this weekend," she said, hoping to get another date with him on the calendar. "And you'll bring lunch."

"You don't even know what it'll be," he said.

"Then tell me your favorite sandwich." She stirred together her toppings, watching as the cheese melted into the hot soup.

"It's a spam and egg salad sandwich," he said, and Cami jerked her attention back to him.

"You're right. That doesn't sound good at all."

He tipped his head back and laughed, the sound magical in Cami's ears. She joined him, shaking her head. "I didn't mean that to be mean."

"It's fine," he said. "Just wait until you try it. I know it sounds weird, but it's *so* good."

She almost wanted to take his word for it. Instead she said, "Great. Can't wait until Saturday." Then she dipped her spoon into her bowl and took a bite of her favorite soup. "Mm," she moaned, and Clay chuckled again.

They chatted easily about the new irrigation project, and Clay's dog, and even a little bit about their evening last night with her siblings.

"That wasn't too weird?" she asked.

"Why would it be weird?" he asked.

Cami shrugged, though she'd laid awake in bed last night, hoping Clay had enjoyed himself. "I don't know. I don't normally integrate my...." She didn't know how to continue, and she looked at Clay.

He simply watched her, that big, white cowboy hat perched perfectly on his head. She looked away as heat filtered through her.

"Boyfriend?" he asked, and Cami's gaze flew back to his.

"Sure," she said, though her voice scratched coming out. "I don't normally bring men back to the homestead quite so early in a relationship."

"I thought it was fun," he said. "And your mother's ice cream is *fantastic*."

"Oh, I see," she said, hoping to lighten the mood. "You came just for the ice cream."

He laughed again, scraping the bottom of his bowl for his last bite of broth. He ate it and grinned at her. "The ice cream wasn't the best part," he said.

"No?" Cami asked, feeling daring and bold. "What was?" They hadn't kissed, though Cami had been thinking about that too. In fact, it was a miracle she'd slept at all last night, what with the way her mind had been zooming around until the wee hours of the morning.

"I don't know," he said. "Maybe holding your hand. Or maybe that kiss on my cheek."

"That was this morning, cowboy," she said, her eyes dropping to his mouth. Pure desire dove through her, and she looked into Clay's eyes again.

But he was looking at her mouth too, and he cleared his throat as he brought his eyes level with hers. They leaned toward one another, and Cami let her eyes drift closed, her heart pounding in the back of her throat.

"...it's in here," Rhodes said, the door opening as he entered.

Clay jumped away from Cami, standing and picking up their empty soup bowls, seemingly in the blink of an eye.

Rhodes glanced at them. "Hey, guys," he said. "Things going okay?"

"Great," Cami squeaked as Clay escaped. She felt red from the tips of her ears to the bottom of her feet, but her brother rummaged around in his desk, came up with something, and left. He didn't pull the door closed, and Clay didn't come back into the office.

Cami leaned back in her chair and tried to find him out in the kitchen, but she couldn't see anyone. The noise had gone down, which meant people had eaten and left already.

She needed to do the same, and she pushed away from her desk, leaving the payroll spreadsheet she'd been working on.

Betsy stood at the sink, rinsing bowls. "Let's go get a massage today," Cami said. "My shoulders are tight from sitting at the computer."

Her sister looked at her. "I bet they are." She wore a sparkle in her eyes that made Cami squirm.

"What does that mean?"

"It means you're all tight because of a certain cowboy, not your computer." Betsy's eyebrows went up.

"No," Cami said quickly, though she wasn't sure why she was denying it. She'd never hidden her feelings for the cowboys she went out with.

"I'm not going if you're not going to tell me about Clay," Betsy said. "And we have to invite Georgia. She's feeling left out of things here at the ranch."

"That's because she's not going to live here much longer," Cami said, the weight of the words heavier than they'd been in the past.

"None of us are," Betsy said, her eyes turning sad. She stopped working, almost like she'd just realized how many changes were coming to the ranch. To their branch of the Quinn family.

So many cousins had experienced similar things, with weddings and babies already for some of Cami's cousins. She'd loved attending the weddings, because that occasion always called for new shoes.

She loved baby showers, because she got to eat cake. As she thought about her own future, she hoped she'd have the ultimate pair of new shoes for her own wedding, and the cake and cookies at her own baby shower.

Does Clay want children? she thought, and she turned away from Betsy. "How are the wedding plans coming?"

"Mine are almost done," she said. "It's Georgia that's been having problems. I think that's why she feels disconnected from us."

"No," Cami said. "It's because she's been spending more time out at that ranch Logan bought." Which she should be, as she'd be living there and running things with him once they got married in November.

"The wedding is only six weeks away," Betsy said quietly, and Cami knew her sister would miss Georgia the most.

Cami put her arm around Betsy and said, "And then yours is only six weeks after that." Their eyes met, and panic ran through Betsy's eyes.

"You're right."

"Hey, you have a handsome fiancé who loves you," Cami said. "Don't worry." She swallowed back a quick jaunt of jealousy, determined not to compare herself to her siblings. Wasn't that was Pastor Dahl had just said last night?

She smiled at her sister. "I'm calling Georgia right now. I've got to get out of the homestead for a little bit this afternoon."

"Okay," Betsy said, bending to load the dishwasher. "I'm in, as long as you talk about Clay."

"Deal," Cami said, deciding to invite Jessie too. She wouldn't come, as she didn't like getting a massage. But Cami did, and she'd call Raina too and find out if the three of them could have a massage in the same room. Her cousin would let them do that, if they had enough massage therapists to staff three appointments at once.

Please, Cami prayed as she dialed Georgia first. She really needed a girly afternoon with her family to get her mind in the right place concerning Clay and their budding relationship.

CHAPTER EIGHT

*C*lay pulled up to the organic farm and parked beside another truck. Carter Quinn grew the best fruits and vegetables in the county, and Clay liked to come out to the farm and get a few things a couple times a month.

They'd deliver too, but since Clay didn't exactly make a meal plan, he never knew what to order or when. But he knew that he wanted to ask Cami to come to dinner tomorrow night, and he wanted to make a grilled chicken Waldorf salad that his one and only college girlfriend had taught him to make.

He hadn't made it for a while, but he knew Carter would have the lettuces and fruit he needed to make the salad a success. It was mostly a lot of chopping—and the grilling of a chicken breast—and he felt confident he could pull it off.

He wasn't sure why he wanted to impress Cami with his culinary skills, especially because he didn't have many of those. Seemed like he should try to win her over with his muscles or his ability to train a dog, because he honestly wasn't sure what would win over Camille Quinn. She'd been out with a lot of cowboys, and maybe she didn't know herself what she wanted.

"Hey, Clay," Carter said, coming out of the small barn where he sold his organic produce. "What are you looking for?"

How to impress a pretty woman, he thought, wondering how Carter had won over Avery. "Kale," he said. "And something else that would be good in the Waldorf salad."

"We have apples," he said, turning to go back inside. "And I've probably got a few other things you'd like."

Clay certainly hoped so, because he'd snuck off the ranch to make this produce run. He needed a break from the work he normally did, and when he got back, he'd make sure Trooper got his play time. Though the dog got out of the house plenty as he worked on the farm with Clay and the other cowboys, Clay liked to make sure Trooper got his ball-chasing in for the day.

And then he needed to get Cami by five so they could get to town and have dinner before the fireside that evening.

He picked out apples, potatoes, lettuces, herbs, and toma-toes before getting back in his truck and hurrying back to the ranch. He ran down the road with Trooper and threw the ball out into the grassy fields. The dog barked to himself, almost a private, personal encouragement to keep looking for that ball until he found it, which made Clay smile.

He'd gone through his list of things to accomplish in a day, though he hadn't done much for safety. Not getting injured counted, he supposed, but he actually wondered if he was risking his safety by going out with Cami.

After all, the woman definitely had the ability to stomp on his heart.

"Hey," she said, and he turned toward her, surprise picking up his pulse and dropping it quickly.

"What time is it?" he asked. He was supposed to pick her

up at five, and while he'd been pressed for time, he hadn't lost track of too much time...had he?

"Four-something," she said. "I was out here giving something to Gil, and I saw you come this way." She smiled at him, and Clay glanced back down the road toward the row of cabins. He couldn't see anyone, and he easily received Cami into his arms as she neared him.

"I still need to shower," he said, his pulse suddenly hammering in his chest. "I was just going to head back."

"Great." She smiled up at him. "We can walk together. I'll hurry back to the homestead and change while you shower."

Trooper barked, startling Clay, and he stepped away from Cami to pick up the ball and throw it again. Then he took Cami back into his arms. He wanted to kiss her before their date that night, and he liked the way Cami traced her fingernails along the back of his neck.

Her eyes drifted closed, and Clay took that as her permission to kiss her.

So he swiped his cowboy hat off his head and pressed it against her back as he lowered his mouth to hers. He didn't waste time with a tease or a touch but kissed her like he'd been thinking about doing for months now.

She gripped his shoulders and kissed him back, and Clay's nerves quieted. He pulled back a few seconds later. "I haven't kissed anyone in a while," he whispered.

"Who was the last woman you kissed?" she asked, her lips catching on his as she kissed him again.

Clay didn't want to answer, though he wasn't embarrassed and had nothing to hide. No, he didn't want to answer, because that meant he'd have to stop kissing Cami, and he didn't want to do that.

So he didn't, and kissing Cami easily the best part of his day, and he hoped he could add it to his daily list of must-do's.

Clay floated through the walk back to his cabin, the conversation between him and Cami easy. He wasn't sure if falling was supposed to be easy, but this relationship felt so simple. She left him with a sly smile and the ghost of her fingers in his so he could shower.

He worried through soaping up and rinsing off. Maybe Cami didn't want simple. "She probably shouldn't date so many cowboys then," he said into the spray, deciding he needed to stop obsessing about everything.

She'd kissed him, and she'd sure seemed to like that—and him. He knew better than most that relationships and situations could be made into something more than they were with too much mental energy. Every person saw things differently, and from Clay's experiences with his brothers, he knew perspective made a huge difference.

They didn't think anything of him leaving Wyoming. Didn't think they needed to invite him to be part of their ranch operations there. Simply didn't think of him.

His chest pinched, where his heart struggled to beat. The moment passed quickly, as they always did when it came to his family, and Clay combed his hair and set his cowboy hat in place. Feeling whole now, with his belt buckle, cowboy boots, and cowboy hat in place, he drew in a deep breath and checked on Trooper's water.

"Need more, bud?"

The dog lay on the floor near the air conditioning vent, his tongue still hanging out of his mouth as he continued to pant. Clay chuckled at his friend, refilled the water bowl, and added a handful of ice because he knew the dog liked to chomp on it.

Sure enough, Trooper dragged himself to his feet and

went over to the bowl, which clunked as the ice cubes hit the sides. He lapped the fresh water and grabbed an ice cube.

"I'll be back later," Clay said, picking up his keys and heading outside to his truck. He'd started the ignition and buckled his seatbelt when his phone rang. Rhodes.

He tapped on the infotainment screen. "Hey, boss," Clay said easily, able to drive and talk, as his phone connected to his truck's Bluetooth.

"Can I talk to you after the fireside tonight?" Rhodes asked.

Clay frowned, his stomach swooping for some reason. "Sure," he said, his voice maybe a bit strained. "What about?"

"We've got a cake house out on the ranch I want to move for the new irrigation system. I'm going to use it to house the machinery, and I need your help coordinating the move."

Relief flowed through Clay. He should've known Rhodes would call about work. He'd been better since starting a romance with Capri, but the man still worked a ton. Clay would too, if he owned a ranch like Quinn Valley.

Maybe that's why your brothers don't have time for you, he thought, unsure of why his brothers had been on his mind so much lately. Perhaps he should reach out, touch base with them, find out how they were doing.

"Yeah, sure," Clay said. "I didn't know we had a cake house on the ranch."

"Yeah, Gramps actually built it," Rhodes said. "I want to involve him too, because it's obviously special to him."

"No problem. We'll be back, oh, I don't know. Probably by nine or so."

"Great, I'll take a nap now." Rhodes laughed, and Clay couldn't help smiling too. He stifled his own yawn as the call ended and he pulled up to the homestead. He took a moment to admire the new landscaping, the impressive home the Quinn's had built and maintained.

Would Cami want to be with someone who didn't have a ranch of their own? He knew Logan Locke had bought his own ranch and would whisk her sister away to it once they were married. Flynn had bought his old family farm where he'd been raised. Knox had a place in town and jobs all over the county, as he was the premier farrier in these parts.

And of course, Rhodes was set to take over the ranch—both physically and on paper—by the New Year. He'd move into the homestead in January, and marry Capri in April.

So where did that leave Cami?

She came out the front door, and Clay jumped out of the truck. "Sorry," he said as he approached her. She wore a pretty white dress with bright splashes of flowers on it. "I got lost inside my head for a second."

Cami smiled and giggled, running the last few steps to him. He caught her in his arms, laughing with her. "What were you thinking about?" she asked.

"You," he said, leaning down to touch his lips to hers in a sweet kiss. "And where you're going to live once Rhodes takes over." He swayed with her, watching that pretty smile fade slightly.

"I'm staying in the basement," she said. "Rhodes said he doesn't need the whole house right away."

Clay sobered too, hoping his questions didn't ruin their evening. "And you'd be...satisfied with a cowboy like me?"

"Like you?" She threaded her fingers through his and tugged him toward the truck.

"Yeah," he said, going with her. "You know, a cowboy without a place of his own. I'm not sure those cabins out on the east end are meant for families." He opened the passenger door and looked at her, eyebrows cocked.

"Oh," she said, their eyes meeting for a long, charged moment. "I guess I hadn't thought about it."

"Hmm," he said, smiling. "I don't think that's true." He

waited for her to climb up and then he closed the door and went around to his side. "Do you want kids?"

"Yeah, sure," she said. "In time. I'm still pretty young." She looked at him. "Do you?"

"I don't know," he said honestly, leveling his gaze at her again. "What if the answer is no? Is that a deal-breaker for you?"

"I don't know," she responded, looking thoughtful now. She focused out the windshield. "I think the only deal-breaker for me is dishonesty. I've had a lot of...issues with that with my previous boyfriends."

"Oh, is that what I am?" Clay teased, because he needed to get this conversation onto something lighter.

"Yeah," Cami said with a light laugh. She slid across the seat and sat next to him. "That's what you are."

"Mm." Clay pressed his lips to her temple and got the truck rolling toward town. Neither of them spoke, and Clay let his thoughts wander wherever they wanted to go. He'd never felt a strong calling toward fatherhood, because he didn't want to be the kind of dad his had been. All he could do was be honest with Cami—and hope that if he came to the conclusion that kids weren't in his future, that she wouldn't end things with him because of it.

CHAPTER NINE

*C*ami's thoughts barely seemed to stay in her mind long enough to think them. *Boyfriend. Kids. A cowboy like me.*

She hadn't expected any serious questions like those until much later in their relationship. Of course, she'd never really kissed a man as quickly as she had Clay either. Never felt as comfortable with one as fast as she had him. Never felt like she could be who she truly was so readily.

She wasn't sure if that was because she'd known him for three years. Or because Jessie and Rhodes both spoke so highly of him. Or if he was her soulmate. The romantic in her wanted it to be the last one, and she curled her fingers around his and squeezed.

"What are you thinking about?" he asked.

"Too much." She took a deep breath. "What do you think Pastor Dahl will talk about tonight?"

"I have no idea."

"I wanted to be a pastor once," she said, smiling out the front window as Clay turned into the parking lot of the one and only Italian restaurant in town. How she'd missed the twenty-five-minute drive to town, she wasn't sure.

Lost in thought.

"Really?" Clay asked, surprise right there in the syllables.

"Yeah." She giggled. "It's a far cry from accounting, right?"

"Like, opposite sides of a canyon." After parking, he twisted to face her. "So why did you choose accounting?"

"Numbers make sense," she said matter-of-factly. "They line up. They don't lie."

"And religion doesn't make sense or line up? It lies?"

"No," she said quickly. "But there are gray areas. Things I don't understand. Things I believe, but don't know." She looked at him, almost desperate for him to agree with him. "Don't you think?"

His eyes softened, and he nodded. "Yeah," he said. "Sometimes we just have to take a step into the dark. That's what my mom always said."

The moment felt heavy for one, two, three breaths, and then they seemed to breathe in together. "Okay," he said, his voice bright now. "Let's go eat. I believe you said pasta was one of your favorite foods."

"And Caprese salad," she said. "With a lot of balsamic vinegar."

"Yes." He grinned at her and got out of the truck, turning back to help her down. She let her palms slide up his arms and across his chest before her feet hit the ground. "You look amazing, by the way," he said, leaning down and kissing her again.

This time, it wasn't just a chaste touch of his lips against hers. But a *kiss*, the way he'd captured her mouth on the lane that ran in front of his house, dead-ending near a stand of trees and that field with long grass.

"I sure do like you, Miss Cami," he murmured, and Cami kept her eyes closed as she smiled, her forehead pressed against his. The other cowboys she'd dated didn't normally say such things to her, and it was just one more reminder that Clay Martin wasn't like the other cowboys she'd dated.

"I like you too, Clay," she whispered, because she was afraid if she gave too much voice to the words, the true strength of her feelings would come out. And they were stronger than she wanted to admit right now, at least out loud.

"Let's go eat," he said. "I'm starving, and we don't want to be late for the fireside."

"No, we don't," she said. "Otherwise, I might have to sit by another cowboy who has a whole row to himself."

Clay laughed, slung his arm around her waist, and pulled her into his side as they walked toward the entrance. "That was just serendipity," he said. "Or dumb luck."

"Fate," she said. "I don't know how Granny got the time wrong for the fireside."

"She didn't," Clay said. "The pastor just started early. He said he wanted to hear the choir do a few numbers. You didn't really miss much."

Oh, Cami had missed something, but she honestly didn't care. They'd gotten a seat, and she'd gotten a new boyfriend. It wasn't the first fall fireside service where she'd left with the hope of a new man in her life, but as she sat across the table from Clay, that handsome face and broad shoulders and beautiful spirit beaming back at her, she actually wanted it to be the last time.

And she had no idea what to do with that idea. It flitted away from her before she could seize onto it and examine it. She let it go, because there would be plenty of time to analyze everything once the date ended.

After all, she didn't need to sleep.

"So REMEMBER, SURROUND YOURSELF WITH PEOPLE WHO can help you see what you cannot...yet." The preacher smiled out at the congregation, and Cami marveled at how he seemed to have everything figured out.

Of course, he didn't. But he'd told some great stories about how he'd come to his own personal testimony of God. Cami was only half his age, and he'd already warned against expecting to have everything figured out while she was yet young.

Clay seemed as invested in the sermon as she was, and Pastor Dahl finished a few minutes later.

"Short," Clay whispered, and Cami nodded as the choir got up. They proceeded to sing several numbers, so by the time the entire service ended, it hadn't been any shorter than the others in the series.

The congregation was invited to sing the closing hymn with the choir, and Cami mouthed the words so she could listen to Clay's beautiful singing voice. No sooner had amen been said when he turned to her. "You didn't sing."

"You have such a great voice," she said, smiling up at him. "I like listening to you."

"My grandmother always said that." He beamed down at her and then turned to leave the pew. Cami caught his hand so they wouldn't get separated in the crowd, and she turned when someone else touched her other hand.

"Cami," a woman said, and Cami turned to see her cousin Riley standing there. Of course, she'd be here. Her husband was one of the preachers.

"Oh, hi, Riley." Cami glanced back at Clay, but there wasn't room for them to walk side-by-side. Maybe she could escape introducing him to Riley, though he'd probably met her at one of the regular Quinn family functions.

"Is he your new boyfriend?" Riley whispered, though

Cami felt like she'd pulled out a microphone and shouted into it.

"Yes," Cami said.

"You seem to have a lot of those."

Cami's eyes cut over to her cousin, but she had no idea what to say. Riley didn't seem to have realized that she'd pushed a button—and she definitely hadn't meant to make Cami's heart thump quite so hard. At least Cami had never known Riley to be anything but kind. Maybe a bit blunt. But not unkind.

Cami supposed she did date a lot of men. She liked having her options open, and she hadn't really thought about settling down until the last couple of months. She'd been in the dating pool long enough to know what she liked now, and what she didn't like.

But seeing her siblings and a vast majority of her cousins find the perfect match for them had helped her see she wanted that too. Her perfect match. And if she had to date a lot of men to find that person, she would.

"Anyway, he looks nice," Riley said, peeling off after they reached the lobby. They probably had dinner set up for the preachers somewhere, and Cami stepped over to Clay.

"Who was that?" Clay asked. "I feel like I've seen her around."

"Yeah, one of my cousins," Cami said, Riley's words moving through her like an infection. She pushed the words out of her mind, because she didn't want them to taint her time with Clay.

She caught him yawning, and she pulled back on the idea to stop and grab a treat somewhere. He didn't suggest it either, which meant he was tired and needed to get to bed. They talked about the sermon on the way back to the ranch, and Clay finally said, "I think I need to talk to my brothers."

Shock lifted Cami's eyebrows. "Oh. What—why?"

"I don't know," he said. "I've been thinking about them a lot lately, and the fireside just now had a good message."

"About surrounding yourself with people who can influence you for the best," she said. "I thought...." She wasn't sure what she thought. She only knew one side of the story with him and his family—and it was his.

"Maybe they'll have something that can help me." He shrugged, and Cami watched the indecision roll across his face. "I don't know."

"What are you hoping for help with?"

"I don't know," he said, but Cami was sure he did. "They have ranches and wives and families." He left his statement there, and Cami let the silence into the truck with them. She thought it would be awkward, but it wasn't, and Cami realized that another difference between Clay and the other cowboys she'd dated existed.

With Malcolm, she'd had to stuff every second with sound. With Gideon, he didn't like silence, and he'd fill it with music and lyrics. With Connor, only awkwardness would accompany them if they weren't talking. Cami didn't want to have to carry a conversation or have one that didn't need to be had.

Clay turned onto the road that led to the homestead, easing to a stop in front of Rhodes's cabin. "I need to talk to your brother for a few minutes," he said. "Do you want me to drop you off first?"

"Is it a privileged conversation?"

Clay chuckled and turned into the driveway. "Hardly. He wants to give me more work to do."

"Well, you are the second," Cami teased, thinking maybe he would have a place right here on this ranch for a while to come.

He scoffed. "I'm not sure I want to be the second," he said. "Foreman. Whatever."

"Are you just saying that?" Cami asked as he turned off the truck. "Because it's okay to love your job."

Clay met Cami's gaze, and something stormed in his eyes. "Yeah, okay. I do love this job, and this ranch."

She grinned at him. It was okay to be who he was. And okay that she was who she was, even if she did date a lot of men.

"I've been out with a lot of cowboys," she said, unsure of where she was going with this new topic.

Clay blinked, obviously as unsure as her. "I know, Cami," he said, and the sound of her name in that voice was absolute magic. "I have eyes." He grinned at her and opened the door. "Let's go see if Rhodes has anything good to eat. He's always bragging about eating ice cream every night."

Cami laughed, determined not to spend another moment worrying about what Riley had said. No, she needed her mental energy for much more important things—like how to keep a good cowboy like Clay interested for longer than a couple of days.

He didn't seem like the type to disappear when the shiny exterior of a project wore off, and she could only hope that was true with women too.

CHAPTER TEN

*C*lay woke the next morning and didn't immediately go to work in the stables. It felt odd and foreign to report to the shop instead, where Rhodes, Gil, Wyatt, and Gramps had already congregated.

"Am I late?" he asked, glancing around.

"Just got here," Rhodes said. "But we're set. Should we head out?"

"Yep," Gil said, pulling a pair of work gloves on before he headed for the backhoe.

"We need heavy machinery?" Clay asked. His meeting with Rhodes the night before had lasted fifteen minutes, and most of that had been because he'd taken forever to scoop the pistachio ice cream.

He'd just wanted Clay to meet at the shop at seven, and they'd be driving out on the ranch to the cake house where they'd pick it up and move it. The forklift had been taken out last night, Rhodes had said. So Clay wasn't aware they needed a backhoe.

"There are poles around the building," Rhodes said.

"Poles? Why would you put poles around a building?" Clay asked.

"Keeps the wind from blowin' it down," Gramps said. "Set them poles myself."

Clay grinned at the older man, and he followed Rhodes and Gramps to Rhodes's brand-new pickup truck. It was bright red, sported a king cab, air conditioned and heated seats, and the best shocks Rhodes could get on a vehicle.

Clay had ridden in it a couple of times, and it was a nice ride. He helped Gramps into the passenger seat of the truck, and he said, "I can't wait until we get back. Betsy is making that cherry limeade I like."

Clay's own mouth watered at the thought. "I forgot Betsy was making this move into an event."

"Pineapple upside down cake," Rhodes added. "Steak and eggs. All of Gramps's favorites."

And Clay's, and his stomach grumbled at him for only drinking coffee before he left his cabin. With him in the back seat, Rhodes started out onto the ranch. The drive was long and bumpy, and by the time they arrived at the cake house— traditionally used to store meat—Clay was ready to get the job done and get back to his regular ranch life.

They set about hooking up the poles to the backhoe, removing them from the stubborn earth one at a time. Gramps told stories of driving to town when he was only twelve years old to get ice cream and candy at the general store.

Gramps had a story for everything, and Clay found himself basking in the tradition and history of the ranch. Suddenly, the day became about much more than just getting a job done. Clay liked the feeling at this ranch, and he wanted to stay here for a good long while.

He should probably say something to Rhodes about it. His boss hadn't said a word about Clay's relationship with his little sister, though he generally frowned on his cowboys dating his sisters. He definitely hadn't been happy when Cami had gone out with Malcolm, and yet Rhodes hadn't said anything about Clay and Cami.

He didn't need to bring it up now, not in front of others, and maybe not until he and Cami really were serious. Although he felt deep things for Cami, he knew that had to be reciprocated for anything real to happen.

"How'd you meet your wife?" Clay asked, and he noticed Rhodes perking up a bit too. He tied the rope to the last pole, but he was definitely listening.

"Oh, I was about to ship out with the Navy," he said. "And there was a big dance. I met her there, and I just knew I was going to marry her."

Clay smiled as the older man chuckled. "It took a few years—and some quick maneuvering on my part—but I got her."

"Maneuvering?" Rhodes asked, pulling on the rope.

"She had another beau while I was gone," Gramps said, shaking her head. "I had to break that up from across the ocean." He laughed again, and Rhodes joined in. "And we know how opinionated Granny is."

"Is she though?" Rhodes asked. "Maybe you're the one who inspired her matchmaking obsession."

Gramps chuckled, and Clay kept his head down. "Oh, she just wants her grandchildren to be happy."

Had Granny been the one to point Cami toward him? And so what if she had?

Clay wasn't sure how he felt about any of it, so he kept his mouth shut and his hands moving. Finally, the building was ready for the forklift, and Clay got back in the truck to head back to the epicenter of the ranch.

The cake house would make its way slowly there, and Rhodes had a special place picked out for it near the smithy.

Apparently, that was where all the mechanics for the new irrigation system would be.

Everyone piled into the house, where the scent of fried eggs and the hint of lime hung in the air. "They're back," Betsy said from a spot at the stove, and the other Quinn sisters got up from the couch in the living room.

Activity bustled through the homestead, and Clay ducked down the hall to the bathroom to wash his hands. When he came out, Cami met him at the end of the hall.

"How'd it go out there?" she asked, running her hands up his arms.

"Just fine," he said, a struggle starting inside him. "Hey, did your grandmother set us up?"

"What?" she asked, but something flickered in her gaze.

"Rhodes said she had a matchmaking ability, and Gramps said she just wants her grandkids to be happy." Clay waited, though the crowd in the kitchen had gone silent. They were probably praying, which meant it was almost time to eat. His stomach pinched with want of food, but he really wanted to hear what Cami had to say as well.

"I mean, she suggested I might meet someone at the fall fireside series," Cami said. "But she didn't say who. And she certainly didn't plan for you to have empty seats by you."

"But she was late to that first fireside," he said.

"I've met other men at the firesides," Cami said. "Granny didn't have anything to do with us sitting by each other. Besides." She looked flustered as she backed up a step. "You'd already asked me out weeks ago. We'd just never set anything up."

Shame dove through Clay. "Okay." He started to step around her but paused when he stood directly beside her. "And Cami, I don't think I want kids."

He watched a perfect storm of emotions roll across her face. "You don't think or you don't?"

"I don't," he said.

"Okay," she said, taking the news in stride. "Thanks for being honest with me."

Clay didn't know how else to be, but he heard someone say his name from the other room. "We should...." He nodded toward the kitchen, and Cami spun around.

"Yeah," she said as she walked away.

Clay wasn't sure why he'd caused a problem. Did it really matter if her grandmother had set them up? And why had he told her now, of all times, that he didn't want kids?

He sighed, unsure about so many things at the moment. But he put a smile on his face and joined everyone in the kitchen. He was hungry and thirsty, and if there was something better than the tart, sweet cherry limeade Betsy put in front of him, he didn't want to know about it.

THAT EVENING, HE HELD HIS PHONE TO HIS EAR WHILE Trooper rooted around in the field for his ball. "Find it, bud," he called to the dog, almost hoping his brother wouldn't answer the phone.

"Hey," Joe said. "Clay?"

"Yeah, hey," he said, his pulse skipping over itself. He wasn't even sure why he was calling.

"Everything okay?" Joe asked.

"Yeah." He cleared his throat. "It's just been a while. I was thinking about you and Jerry...and everyone. How are things?"

"Things are fine," Joe said, a hint of surprise in his words. "The wives are good. Kids are growing like weeds, but finally able to help out a little bit on the ranch."

Clay pictured his oldest brother, who'd been married for over a decade now. He and his wife, Tammy, had two kids. And Jerry had three with his wife, Flo.

"Great," Clay said.

"What about you?" Joe asked. "How are things in...Idaho?"

At that moment, Clay realized his brother didn't even know where he lived. "Good," he said anyway, the word scraping the back of his throat. "Great."

"Are you seeing anyone?" Joe asked, a normal question. But the words were stale. Uninteresting.

And Clay didn't want to tell his brother anything about Cami. Joe didn't get a seat at his table; he didn't get to know all the intimate details of his life.

So he said, "Nope," and pressed his lips together. Out in the field, Trooper barked, dove for the ball, and came up with it. "Look, I have to go."

"Oh, okay," Joe said.

"Talk to you later." Clay hung up quickly, finally releasing the breath that was stuck in his chest. Trooper dropped the ball, all four feet already shuffling in anticipation of Clay throwing it again.

Clay looked at the dog, and he felt a keen sense of sadness that he loved this dog more than his brothers loved him. "All right, bud," he said, bending to pick up the slobbery, slightly muddy ball. "Go find it."

He launched the ball out in the field and watched Trooper streak after it. He repeated the activity for a while—longer than normal—because he didn't want to return to his cabin alone.

At the same time, he was immensely grateful he was alone, because then he wouldn't snap at anyone who didn't deserve it.

Back home, he got Trooper fresh water and washed his hands, his mind churning and chewing through the events of the day. He was mentally and emotionally exhausted, and he went down the hall to his bedroom.

Dropping to his knees, he looked up at the ceiling. "Dear Lord," he said, his voice hoarse. "Help me. Do I need to do more with Joe and Jerry? Or just let things be?"

A sense of calm came over him, and he realized he didn't need to change anything between him and his brothers. Just because the Quinns had a tight family unit didn't mean he had to.

He could belong to theirs.

"And what about Cami?" he prayed, allowing his neck to bend as he bowed his head. "I really don't want children." He knew that now. "Does that make me selfish?" he whispered. "A bad person?"

He just didn't see himself as a dad, and he didn't want to mess up and have kids who turned out like him.

The only thing circling in his mind now was to *talk to Cami*. So he got up off the hard ground—his bones creaky and complaining—and reached for his phone.

What are you thinking about what I said in the hall today? Before he could chicken out, he sent the text.

I don't know, her response came. *Still processing.*

Clay sighed, though he supposed she did need time to work through a statement like, "I don't want children."

Everyone in the Quinn family seemed to want children— and a lot of them. Cami had four siblings. Her father had four siblings. Her father's father had four siblings. A handful of children seemed to come with the last name.

He couldn't think through things inside the cabin, so he went outside and sat on the back steps to watch the sun go down in the west.

There was another fireside in the series tomorrow night, and he and Cami had made plans to attend them all together. Would she even want to go with him now?

I'm watching the sun set from my back porch, he sent to her. *If you want to come watch with me, you can.*

She didn't respond, and Clay didn't know what to make of the silence. He did know how to stroke his dog and watch as the sky turned gold and then red. All he could do was hope and pray Cami hadn't broken up with him without saying anything at all.

CHAPTER ELEVEN

*I*f Cami drove to Clay's, he'd hear her coming. And if she didn't drive, she'd miss the sunset. Tired of the battle that had been raging within herself since the crew had returned from moving the cake house, she grabbed a set of keys for the ATV and headed outside.

"Where are you going?" Jessie asked, but Cami didn't respond.

She'd straddled the machine and started it when her sister came running down the steps toward her. Jessie was as strong-willed as she was, and Cami should've known she wouldn't just let her drive off into the night.

"Hey," Jessie said, concern on her face. "You've been acting weird today."

Cami couldn't even deny it. She'd been distracted all afternoon, and she'd finally told her mother she wasn't feeling well and gone down to her bedroom.

"I don't know," she said. "It's just Clay."

"Is he not being nice? Because I will march right over there myself, and—"

"He's nice," Cami said. "That's not it." She didn't want to

get into details with Jessie, especially given her sister's friendship with Clay.

"Hey, look," Jessie said, and Cami looked at her older sister. "I know you don't want to talk about him with me. But it's okay. You work through things with me, then you go work *on* them with him." She smiled gently. "You know, if you like him enough to do that."

Cami nodded. "I think I do."

"Then what's the big deal? You've only been seeing him for a few days."

A few days. Had it really only been a few days? It felt like so much longer to Cami, and in a good way.

"He doesn't want kids." Cami closed her eyes in a long blink. She wasn't sure what part of her went up in smoke with those words, but maybe it wasn't all of her. Maybe she didn't need children to be fulfilled.

"Oh, you're talking about kids already." Jessie nodded in a bobbly sort of way, like that was a totally normal conversation to be having after only a few days.

"Yeah," Cami said. "And he's got a bit of a rough past with his family, and he told me today he doesn't want kids."

"And?" Jessie asked.

"And I don't know. He invited me to come watch the sunset with him, and I thought I would. See how I feel when I'm with him." She already knew how she felt with him. Safe. Cherished. Loved.

"Well, you better get going," Jessie said, looking up into the sky. "It's almost gone."

"I'll check in with you when I get back," Cami said.

Jessie fell back a few steps. "All right. Try to have fun."

Cami smiled at her sister and turned the ATV in a wide arc, aiming it east to get to the row of cabins on the horizon.

Clay definitely heard her coming, and he stood on the bottom step when she finally eased the vehicle to a stop. She stepped onto the edge of his grass, nervous energy firing through her with every stride she took.

"You came," he said, somewhat of an awed quality in his voice.

"Yeah." She stepped right into his arms, and all of her cares and worries dried right up. He held her tightly in those strong arms, and she felt like she could face the world and all of its problems as long as he stood at her side.

She twisted and stood beside him, the last light of the day fading in the west. "Gorgeous," she said, because twilight really was beautiful as it draped over the Idaho countryside.

He leaned over and pressed his lips to her temple, and Cami smiled into the night. She turned to kiss him, saying, "I think I'm okay if we don't have kids," she said.

"It's silly for us to decide right now anyway," he whispered back, claiming her lips again. "I mean, we can change our minds later, right?"

Cami just nodded, because if there was something she was very good at, it was changing her mind. She didn't want to lose Clay over the issue of having children or not, because he was the best man she'd dated in the three years she'd been back in Quinn Valley.

Not only that, but maybe she could live here in this cowboy cabin with him if they stayed together. Or in the cabin where Rhodes lived. If it was just the two of them—and Trooper—they didn't need a great big homestead.

The last of the light faded from the sky, plunging them into true country darkness. Clay kept his arms around her, comforting her, and asked, "Do you want to come in and have dinner?"

"You haven't eaten yet?"

"Nope," he said. "I tend to forget to do basic things when I have a lot on my mind." He grinned at her, the Clay she'd been getting to know suddenly right in front of her.

"I'm making a note of that," she said, glad he'd been thinking as hard as she had the past several hours. "And I'd love to see what you can make for dinner."

"Oh-ho," he said. "I think you're going to be surprised." He led her up the back steps and into his house, where he proceeded to get out real produce and make a Waldorf salad, complete with grilled chicken and homemade vinaigrette.

"Wow," she said as she looked at the beautiful, composed salad in the bowl. She lifted her gaze to his. "You really are perfect."

He laughed, and Cami joined in. "It's the one thing one of my girlfriends taught me," he said.

"How many girlfriends have you had?" she asked, spearing a piece of chicken and getting a bite of lettuce and apple too.

"Only a few," he admitted. "This one was the one I had in college for the year I went."

"Well, I thank her." Cami lifted her fork with a bite of salad on it in a toast and then ate her food. "Mm," she said as the tangy salad dressing hit her taste buds. "This is great."

"I think you're great," Clay said, and he took a bite of his own salad. Cami smiled at him as she felt herself slipping a little further in love with him.

She hoped she wasn't falling too fast, but she didn't quite know how to slow down. There was nothing around her to grab onto, and after they finished eating, Clay took her face in both of his hands and kissed her.

By the time she tiptoed back into the homestead, she felt like a teenager trying to sneak past her parents in the middle of the night.

Her phone lit up as she used it as a flashlight to get her down the steps without breaking a bone, and she glanced at it.

Her dad: *Did you just pull up on the ATV?*

Adrenaline forced her heart to pump out several extra

beats. *Yes*, she typed out. *Sorry*. She should've walked or taken a truck that didn't have such a growly motor. Now everyone on the ranch knew where she'd been, and how late she'd been out.

Just making sure, he sent back, and Cami continued downstairs. She took a quick detour into Jessie's room to let her know she'd returned, and then Cami hurried into her own bedroom. With the door closed behind her, she allowed herself to relive the way Clay kissed her and how she kissed him back.

"Thank you," she whispered to God. "Guide me so I don't lose him." She'd never involved the Lord too much in her previous relationships, but Cami found herself needing His help. She wasn't sure what that said about her, or maybe it was about Clay. But she just knew she needed some extra guidance to know if what she was doing was right or not.

She sure hoped a relationship with Clay was right, because she definitely liked him a whole lot. And she suddenly couldn't wait for the fireside the next evening—because she'd get to see Clay again.

A CHILL RAN DOWN CAMI'S ARMS, AND NOT FOR THE FIRST time since walking in the chapel. Pastor Dahl had been talking for twenty minutes, and her attention hadn't wandered once.

Her heart hurt though. Her pulse kept racing and then slowing down. Speeding up and stalling.

Clay put his arm around her and drew her into his body. "You okay?" he asked, seemingly not upset by anything the preacher was saying.

She nodded, but she hadn't been able to let go of one

statement. *Be sure to surround yourself with people who share the same goals, ideals, and values you do.*

She'd been trying to figure out if Clay was that man or not. He seemed to love the firesides. He was hardworking. Loyal. Loved dogs.

But he didn't seem to have the same fondness for family that she did. He didn't want children. And while Cami knew all life decisions didn't have to be made at age twenty-seven, she also felt sure the Lord was trying to tell her something.

Or maybe He wasn't.

Cami honestly didn't know anymore. She'd had a conversation with Clay about religion making sense, and right now, it didn't. She just wanted to be alone and let her mind work through things.

But the pastor spoke for another forty minutes, and by then, her nerves screamed at her to get home and barricade herself in her room.

Clay wasn't in any hurry, though, and he stopped to chat with a couple of cowboys who worked a different ranch. She caught sight of one of her cousins and went to say hello.

"Riley," she said, and her cousin turned toward her.

"Cami." They embraced, and Cami could feel the joy coming off of her.

"How's married life?"

"Oh, a barrel of fun." Riley grinned at Cami and then her new husband, Blake.

"Reverend," Cami said, and they shook hands. "Are you enjoying the fireside series?"

"It's great," he said, linking his arm around Riley. They were just so cute, and Cami had actually enjoyed the double wedding with Riley and Raina. Their branch of the Quinn family certainly knew how to throw a party.

Clay came up to her, and she introduced him to Riley and Blake. Thankfully, Riley didn't say anything about Cami's dating habits, and Cami and Clay were able to make a graceful exit.

She didn't feel like talking on the way back to the ranch, and while the silence between her and Clay had always been comfortable, tonight, it felt different. She felt different.

"Ready for a fireside marathon to end the series?" Clay asked as he pulled up to the homestead. "Friday, Saturday, and Sunday."

"Yeah," she said absently, reaching for the door handle. "See you then." She was so out of it that she didn't notice him getting out of the truck until he met her in front of it.

"What's going on?" he asked.

"What do you mean?" She finally tilted her head back and looked at him. Really looked at him. She didn't want to hurt him, that much was for sure.

"I mean, you've been acting...I don't know. Distant? Weird. Since the fireside. I even asked you something on the way back, and you didn't respond."

"I'm just thinking about what Pastor Dahl said."

"And what's that?" Clay laced his fingers through hers. "He spoke for over an hour tonight."

Cami ducked her head, her auburn curls falling between them. She'd worked so hard on her hair too, because looking her best when she left the house was important to her.

"Cami," Clay said, gently pressing her chin up with his hand. His eyes searched hers, and she honestly had no idea what he found there. She couldn't read anything past the curiosity swimming in his gaze.

"I think we should break up," she blurted just as he opened his mouth to say something.

Shock flowed across his face, and he fell back a step. "You do." He wasn't asking, and he sighed a sound heavy with frustration as he took off his cowboy hat and rubbed his hand through his hair.

"Is this because I don't want kids?"

"No," she said, though that definitely had something to do with it. "Maybe. I'm not sure."

"We don't have to be one-hundred-percent sure right now," he said, narrowing his eyes at her. "Do we?"

"I mean, I don't know." She just wanted someone to tell her what to do. "Maybe I'm just...I don't know. Maybe I just need a break." She'd talked about going on a fast the way Flynn had done, but then there was Clay, waiting for her on the end of the bench.

"You're not making sense," Clay said. "We've only been seeing each other for a few days."

Cami heard what he was saying—*we don't need to break up so soon*—but she needed space and distance to find the clarity she didn't currently have.

Or maybe she didn't.

"I'm sorry," she said, tears pricking her eyes. "I don't know what I want right now, and I just need time to think." She started to walk toward the front porch, and he let her go.

"Time to think," he repeated somewhere behind her. Cami didn't look back, and Clay didn't run after her.

She made it into the house, down the steps, and into her bedroom, tears coating her cheeks the entire way.

CHAPTER TWELVE

*C*lay had no idea what had just happened. One moment, he was enjoying the fireside with his girlfriend, and the next, he didn't even have a girlfriend.

He realized with the snap of the front door closing that Cami had left. And he hadn't said anything.

"Time to think," he said again—he had said that. What did that even mean? Maybe he'd crowded her. Maybe they'd spent too much time together over the last five days. He was emotionally spent as well, but only because a relationship with someone as special as Cami required him to delve into himself and what he really believed and what he really wanted.

He stared at the house until the motion sensor light turned off, and then he realized he couldn't just camp out on the front lawn. Walking to his truck caused the front porch lights to snap back on, and he hurried then. He didn't need anyone to catch him standing there, his heart weeping at what had just happened.

Trooper waited for him at home, and Clay murmured hello to the dog as he wandered down the hall to his bedroom. The stupor lifted, and a rush of anger took its place.

Had Cami been playing with him? He hadn't pegged her for that type of mean woman, though he knew they existed. She sure did burn through a lot of boyfriends, and maybe that was because of *her* and not them.

Clay had always assumed them not good enough for her, because honestly, who was? He didn't feel like he was, and yet...they had shared a powerful connection in the past, especially the last several days.

He wanted to call her, but that wouldn't be giving her time or space. He exhaled heavily as he laid back on his bed, glad when Trooper jumped up, circled, and then laid right against his side.

At least the dog hadn't gone crazy and given up on him before they'd really gotten to know one another.

CLAY KEPT HIS HEAD DOWN THE NEXT MORNING. HE SAW no reason to call attention to himself. He had plenty of chores to do, and he worked steadily through the feeding and care of the animals before going to the barn where Jessie kept track of the herd.

He had a small section of the counter there where he kept his paperwork too, and he stalled outside the barn to send up a prayer that she wouldn't be there. Jessie mostly worked in the barn in the mornings, choosing to spend her afternoons out in the fields, enclosures, and cattle barns. Or with Flynn.

After pushing into the barn, he found her space empty, and pure relief filled him. He just needed to go over Rhodes's plans and figure out what he should be doing now that they'd moved the cake house.

As he flipped pages, he realized he had a meeting that

afternoon with the sprinkler supplier in town. He hurried to check his phone, glad when he still had plenty of time to review what Rhodes wanted, grab lunch, and drive to town.

A drive he was supposed to make with Cami. Rhodes would attend the meeting too, so Clay wouldn't have to be alone with Cami. But he almost thought the three of them would be worse.

Maybe you can get out of it, he thought, swiping to send a text to Rhodes. *Swamped on the ranch today. Can you and Cami handle the supplies?*

Rhodes called, and Clay cursed himself for saying anything. He couldn't ignore the call, as he'd literally just texted. So he opened the line and said, "Hey."

"You're swamped with what?"

Clay had no idea what to say. "I'm not swamped."

"You just don't want to go," Rhodes said matter-of-factly.

"Right."

"Why not? I thought you were excited about this project. It allows us to water three hundred additional acres every year."

And the thought of prepping three hundred more acres to plant made Clay tired. And planting it. And cultivating it. And adding that land to the crop rotation. He sighed. "I am excited about it. I'm just...I'm tired. I didn't sleep well last night." Hey, he wasn't lying.

"And the way my sister has been crying all morning would have nothing to do with this."

"She's been crying?"

"All. Morning," Rhodes said. "At least according to Betsy, and she's not usually overdramatic."

Clay turned toward the barn door as it opened. Jessie came in, and their eyes met. If he hadn't wanted to say anything before—and he hadn't—he definitely wasn't going to now. "I have to go," he said to his boss, and he hung up.

The awkwardness between him and Jessie was so thick it choked him. "Hey," he said anyway, lifting one hand in a ridiculous wave. And she wasn't even Cami. He never should've started a relationship with a Quinn. At least not one where it might not work out.

"Hey, Clay," she said easily, moving toward him so quickly he didn't have time to get out of the way. She drew him right into a hug and asked, "How are you doing?"

He wanted to sigh and soften and tell her everything. In that moment, he realized he didn't have anyone to tell. No one to talk to, or work through things with. And he loved Jessie like a sister.

"Cami broke up with me," he said. "That's how I'm doing."

"Oh, the whole ranch knows," Jessie said, stepping back. "She's not real quiet about things." She gave him a strained smile and tucked her hands in her back pockets. "I'm sorry about her."

"Why are you sorry?"

"She's…still trying to figure out what she wants."

"Seems like she would know by now," Clay said, instantly regretting the words. "I'm sorry. I didn't mean that." He didn't want to talk badly about Cami, not to her sister. Not to anyone.

Jessie smiled more fully at him now. "No, you're right. I won't tell her you said that."

Clay wanted to ask his friend what to do next. But he didn't want to seem desperate, and he didn't want to share more with Jessie than he shared with Cami.

He lifted the folder of equipment they needed for the new irrigation system. "Well, I have to go over this and get to a meeting in town."

"Okay," Jessie said, and she watched him leave the barn.

Once free from the weight of her gaze, Clay drew in a

deep breath. "Okay, Lord," he said. He didn't have anything else to add, and he took his folder of specs to a bench in the shade and started going through it all.

Hours later, he pulled up to Rhodes's cabin, where he'd agreed to meet with his boss. He didn't get out of his truck or text his friend. Rhodes would come out when he was ready, and sure enough, the front door opened a few seconds later. He climbed in the passenger side and said, "All right. Let's go."

"No Cami?"

"I told her she didn't need to come," Rhodes said, keeping his gaze out the passenger window. "Trust me, she's in no state for a meeting anyhow."

"You know she broke things off with me," Clay said. "Not the other way around." He glanced at Rhodes. "Right?"

"Oh, I know," Rhodes said, finally meeting Clay's eye. "Cami is a special woman." He smiled, obviously not going to say any more.

Clay should be—and was—grateful for that. He adjusted the volume on the radio and pulled out of Rhodes's driveway. "So you built that soda wall for Capri."

"No, what I did for Capri was apologize," he said. "Profusely. And I cut back my hours, and I showed her I wanted to spend time with her."

Clay frowned. "I—"

"I'm not sayin' you did anything wrong, Clay," Rhodes said. "What I'm saying is Cami needs to figure some things out. Once she knows what's in her way, she'll come back to you."

Clay's fingers tightened on the steering wheel. He didn't normally need to be reassured quite so much, but he wanted Rhodes to tell him again. He refused to ask though, and instead, focused his attention on the driving.

"There are a few fixes in your orders there," he said, nodding to the folder on the seat between them.

"Fixes?" Rhodes picked up the folder.

"Some of the numbers weren't quite right," he said. "We needed less fittings, for example. And several more sprinkler heads, at least if I read the type of assembly you want correctly."

"Cami did the numbers," Rhodes said, flipping through the pages. "But I'm sure you're right. Her numbers were estimates."

Clay was just glad they were off the fragile ground of talking about Cami. He had nothing but time, and he supposed if Cami needed a little bit of it to figure out how she felt about him, he could give it to her.

If only his chest didn't feel like it was about to cave in on itself.

CHAPTER THIRTEEN

*C*ami sat in the window seat in the dining room, the view out the window to the west showing her the sinking sun. Soon enough, it would be gone, and another day without Clay would be over.

The first day without Clay.

Why did it feel like a lifetime had passed?

Why had she broken up with him?

Betsy had let her stay upstairs in the homestead, though Cami couldn't seem to stop crying. That kind of thing normally annoyed Betsy, but she'd been kind and supportive that day.

Right now, no one was on the main level at the homestead, as they all had significant others to spend their evenings with. Cami wanted to surround herself with people that shared the same goals and morals she did—and that had always been her family.

"Maybe you just panicked," she said to herself. And maybe she had. Maybe she'd allowed herself to get too far into her own head about Clay's reluctance to have children. Family was everything to her, and she couldn't believe she'd told him she was okay being childless.

She wasn't.

He should know that, she thought, and she flipped her phone in her fingers. She'd been toying with the idea of calling him for hours now, but she still hadn't done it. After all, she'd had a boyfriend who'd broken up with her and then contacted her all the time. Jackson's continued reminders of him had annoyed her. Hurt her. Kept wounds open that should've been able to be closed.

She wouldn't do that to Clay. She respected him so much.

A pair of headlights cut through the darkness, and Cami blinked. How long had she been sitting here? Long enough for the sun to go down and she hadn't even noticed.

Car doors slammed, and Cami expected someone to come through the front doors. They didn't, and for some reason, her continued isolation cut through her whole soul. A fresh set of tears started, and she hated that she didn't know how to do anything but cry.

"...get the invitations tomorrow."

She turned toward Georgia's voice, almost wishing she wouldn't snap on the lights. But she did, and Georgia came in with bags in her hands, their mother right behind her.

"And Betsy is using that same photographer," her mom said. "And she said you picked a cake."

Cami kept her knees tucked right to her chest, wondering if they'd even notice her in the window. She'd lived so much of her life in the Quinn family shadows, being one of the younger Quinns in the valley.

"I did," Georgia said. "Mom, it's so amazing. It's the one with seven layers."

Their mother smiled, and set her bags on the counter. "Okay, so we'll start on these table decorations and get every-thing set." She glanced around, and still she didn't see Cami only twenty feet away. "Do you think Betsy would mind us storing them on the table?"

"Yes," Georgia said. "We eat there every weekend, Mom. Maybe we can set up a table in Cami's office."

Her heart leapt at the mention of her name.

"How is she?" their mother asked. "I texted her twice today, but she never answered." She started pulling out white and burgundy craft supplies. "Didn't we get those silver twigs?"

"Yes," Georgia said. "I think I had them." She produced the items their mom wanted, and Cami wished she had such an easy relationship with their mom. But their relationship was simply more business-like, as Cami's mom had been the one to catch Cami up on all the financial matters on the ranch. Their previous accountant had retired before Cami had finished college, and she honestly felt like she'd fumbled in the dark for a solid year after returning to the ranch.

If she were being completely honest with herself, she was still stumbling through life. Completely.

"Cami's...I don't know," Georgia said. "I'm not sure why she broke up with Clay. She probably doesn't even know."

"She does that a lot," her mom said. "Or am I reading that wrong?"

"I don't know," Georgia said. "She's always been the one with the most dates. Maybe she just...." She lifted her shoulders in a shrug. "I don't know. Jessie will know better than anyone." Georgia surveyed the supplies on the counter while Cami's heartbeat thudded in her chest.

It was a completely strange sensation to hear others talk about her, even if they hadn't said anything bad.

"She was my easiest baby," her mom said with such love in her voice. "I finally had a thing or two figured out by the time she came along." She gave a light laugh, and Cami couldn't help the half-sob, half-laugh that came from her mouth too.

Both Georgia and her mother turned toward her, and pure shock filled her mom's face. "Cami." She strode toward her and gathered her right into the motherly embrace Cami needed. She clung to her mother and wept, and her mother stroked her hair and told her everything would be all right.

"He must be something special," her mom finally said, pulling away from Cami. "I mean, he's what? Your fifth boyfriend this year, and I've never seen you cry over one of them."

That wasn't entirely true, but Cami had contained her tears to her bedroom. She got control of herself and sat back against the wall. Georgia brought her a steaming cup of tea, and Cami smiled at her gratefully.

"Tell us what's really going on," her mom said.

Cami took a sip of her tea, trying to get her thoughts aligned. "Clay doesn't want kids."

Her mom swallowed and cut a glance at Georgia. "Okay, well, I wasn't aware you were revving at the starting line to get pregnant."

Georgia giggled, and suddenly Cami found everything funny too.

"What?" their mom asked.

"Well, we didn't get married at twenty-three and have a baby nine months later, no," Georgia said with a smile.

"Everyone has their own path," their mom said with a smile. "I actually wish I'd been older."

Cami sobered and looked at her mom. "Really?"

"I wouldn't change my life for anything," she said. "I love your father. But yes, I got married really young. I haven't done some things that others get to do. I had five kids in nine years, and the ranch and family was my whole life."

"What would've you done?" Georgia asked, and Cami was as equally interested. She'd never heard her mother talk like this.

"Travel," her mom said with a sigh. "Date lots of people."

"I got that one down," Cami said, though a new twinge of pain moved through her.

"Dance more at the weekend celebrations in town," her mom said, tucking Cami's hair. "So if you need some time to figure out what you want, you should take it."

"That's what I told Clay," Cami said. "I just needed some time."

"I did that with Logan too," Georgia said quietly. "If he's a keeper, Cami, he'll be there when you go back."

Cami sighed and looked at her reflection in the dark window.

"But you can't spend any more days crying," her mom said. "You wanted time to figure things out, so you better use it wisely." She got up, her pep talk for the evening obviously done. She sighed too and added, "Can we put these things in the office, dear? The wedding is *so close*."

"Yeah, sure," Cami said. Georgia's wedding was close, and Cami couldn't wait to celebrate in a pretty dress with her family. She'd always have them, even if she never had kids of her own. Maybe that was her path.

When she closed her eyes and pictured who was at her side, no matter what—it was Clay Martin. She already knew they shared the same values and morals. The number of people at the fall firesides dwindled every time there was another one, but Clay had always wanted to go, even more than Cami.

Georgia and her mother started taking the bags of supplies into the office, and Cami leaned her head back and closed her eyes. The back door opened again, and this time Jessie and Betsy entered, talking to each other about that night's poker game. She watched them to see if they'd spot her, and when they didn't, she knew she'd found her new hang out seat. She could literally eavesdrop on everyone from this perch.

"All I'm saying is he looked terrible," Betsy said.

"I know," Jessie said. "But whatever happened is between him and Cami."

"I'm sure he told you *some*thing," Betsy said.

"She's in the window seat," Georgia said, coming back into the room, and all conversation stopped.

Cami raised her hand in a wave, and Jessie and Betsy exchanged a glance. "How was poker tonight?" she asked. "Who'd you go for?"

"Wyatt," Jessie said. "And your boyfriend badgered me to no end."

"You told him you'd coach him," Betsy said. "Remember how he arranged all that transportation of the cattle for you?"

"Yes," Jessie practically shouted, glaring at Betsy. "I just didn't realize I'd need to pay him back so soon."

Cami watched Jessie, because her sister had always had a stronger friendship with Clay than Cami had. She hadn't ever been jealous of her—until that moment. "And?" she asked, her voice almost too sharp.

"And what?" Jessie asked.

"What did he tell you? I agree with Betsy; he must've said something."

"He didn't," Jessie insisted. "He didn't want to say anything bad about you, but he's clearly hurting."

Cami breathed in deeply and nodded. "I wish that weren't true." She got up and started for the stairs that led down to the basement. "I'm going to bed. I'm helping Granny with her ladies' brunch tomorrow morning."

And she still had loads of work to do on top of that.

"I thought those were on Wednesdays," Georgia said, confusion in her voice. Cami didn't answer, because she didn't want to admit that Granny had called and invited just her to brunch tomorrow. She'd surely have something to say about Clay, and Cami thought she better figure some things out quickly, so she'd have some explanations for her grandmother come morning.

"Knock, knock," she said the next morning. "Granny?"

"Coming," the older woman said, and Cami entered the house and closed the door against the crisp autumn morning. The cabin smelled like bacon and onions, and Cami's mouth watered. She wasn't even sure she'd eaten yesterday.

"Something smells good," she said to her grandmother when she came bustling down the hall. "Where's Gramps?"

"He's over doing something with Rhodes," Granny said, smiling at Cami. She enveloped her in a hug. "How are you, dear?"

"Okay," Cami said, because she hadn't cried in ten hours. So, progress.

"How are you enjoying the fireside series?" She turned and went into the kitchen, but Cami's appetite had fled.

"It's...okay," she said. "I don't think I'm going to go anymore."

"There are only three left." Granny peered at her over her shoulder. "What happened?"

"Granny, do you...believe everything the pastor says?"

The way she didn't answer right away was the answer Cami needed. She hunched over to pull the breakfast casserole out of the oven. "I believe," Granny said, tossing the oven mitts onto the counter. "I don't know or understand everything," she continued. "Even at my age."

Cami appreciated her honesty, and she crossed the room to hug her grandmother. "Did you hear him say the other night to surround yourself with people with the same goals and morals as you?"

"Did he?" Granny asked, reaching for the silverware drawer. "Is that why you broke up with that cowboy? The one that was perfect for you?"

A perfect storm raged inside Cami. "We're from two different worlds."

"Oh, well, that's easy to fix," she said. "You marry that cowboy, he'll come around." Her eyes lit up. "I mean, that's what I did to your grandfather."

Cami giggled. "What does that mean?"

"It means that we were the same enough, in all the most important ways. Everything else, dear? It doesn't matter."

"But what are the important ways?" Cami took the plate Granny handed to her, desperate for answers.

"We loved each other," Granny said. "And we were both willing to forgive. That's all that really matters."

Really? Cami wanted to ask, but she didn't. She wasn't in love with Clay—yet. But maybe she had ended things with him a little prematurely. So she needed to talk to him—and find out if he was the forgiving cowboy she hoped he was.

CHAPTER FOURTEEN

Clay knotted his tie, a sigh cutting him to the core. He wanted to attend the fireside tonight, but he also thought getting behind the wheel and driving until he ran out of gas sounded good.

He'd worked all day without running into anyone who'd asked him about Cami. Poker night had been torture enough with two of her sisters there. Not only that, but Jessie hadn't really given him all of her secrets, the way she'd agreed to.

He'd run down the lane with Trooper and thrown the ball. He'd eaten dinner alone and showered, and now he was trying to get himself out to the cab of his truck to get to the fireside. He was dressed. Ready.

He couldn't move.

Trooper barked, looking at Clay like *There's an intruder! Intruder!* He panted as he ran over to the front door and barked some more.

Someone knocked, and it wasn't Cami, though Clay's hopes had soared toward the stratosphere.

"Come on in," Clay called, finally getting his feet to take him out of the mouth of the hallway.

Wyatt and Newt entered, and they both had their church clothes on too. "You're coming to the fireside tonight?" he asked.

"You need a ride, right?" Newt asked.

"No." Clay's brows furrowed. "Why would I need a ride? And you guys never come to the firesides."

"Yeah, well, you met yourself a pretty girlfriend." Wyatt adjusted his tie and puffed out his chest. "And we want to do the same."

Clay laughed, some of it coated in bitterness. "You must not have heard that she broke up with me after only five days." Saying it so bluntly sent a wave of agony through his body. His smile slipped, but he wasn't sure his friends noticed.

"We heard," Newt said. "That's why we're going with you tonight." He gestured for Clay to come with them. "So hurry up. I hear these things fill up."

"You guys really don't have to do this," he said.

"We want to," Wyatt said, pausing in the doorway. "Clay, I know you don't make friends all that easily, but we're your friends."

He was saying so much more than that, and Clay cleared his throat. "Thank you," he said quietly. "I am glad I don't have to go alone." Part of him wanted to be alone. That was his default. But it didn't have to be, and he basked in the chatter and vibes of Wyatt and Newt as they drove the thirty minutes to the church for the service.

Pastor Dahl spoke a bit more about cleansing. Making sure all the negative influences in his life were gone. Only allowing in the good. Clay agreed with him, he did. He just wished he'd been deemed good enough for Cami.

By the time he and Wyatt and Newt spilled back into the night, Newt said, "Whew. You owe me big time for that." He loosened his tie and removed it, practically whipping the person next to him with it.

Clay wasn't sure why, but he found that funny, and he started laughing. And laughing.

"Ah, there he is," Newt said, joining in. "Okay, boys, I'm feeling parched after that. Who's in for a soda at that fancy new shop?"

Clay definitely was, and Wyatt had literally never said no to a soda pop. They headed toward Newt's truck, and Clay didn't even see Cami until Wyatt yelled her name.

Everything stopped in his world, and he lifted his eyes to hers. She stood next to Newt's truck, a perfectly pretty yellow dress swaying in the autumn breeze.

"Oh, boy," Newt said, pausing next to Wyatt. Clay could only stare at the woman, and he had no idea what to say.

"Do you boys mind?" Cami took a step forward. "Can I borrow Clay for a minute? I can give him a ride home."

"I don't know." Newt stepped in front of Clay, as if defending him. "Are you driving that sedan? Because our boy here can't fold his shoulders into a sedan."

"Newt," Clay said, almost under his breath.

"We need him," Wyatt said, joining Newt. The two of them made a human wall between him and Cami, and Clay actually appreciated the gesture. Newt and Wyatt felt like... brothers. Like they'd have his back, no matter the situation.

"Guys," he said.

"I have my sedan, yes," Cami said. "Not all of us drive big, old, smelly trucks." She kicked a grin at the lot of them, and Clay ducked his head and smiled. Her heels clicked against the asphalt as she walked toward them. She put a palm each on Wyatt and Newt and said, "I'll bring him home, boys, good as new. I promise."

"It's okay," Clay said. "Really." He wasn't sure what Cami was going to say, but he wanted to hear it.

"All right," Newt said, a highly dubious quality to his voice. "But you call me if you need something." He gave

Cami a cocked-eyebrow glare, to which she simply smiled at him. He watched Newt and Wyatt get in the truck and drive out of the parking lot, and then he looked at Cami.

"Did you go to the fireside?" he asked.

"Most of it." She clenched her hands together, her nervous energy pouring off of her in waves.

"You don't have to say anything," he said, though he didn't have a ride back to the ranch now.

"I came to say something," she said. "I'm just having a hard time finding the right words."

"Just blurt them out," he said. "Like ripping off a bandage." She'd already done that—two nights ago when she'd announced she didn't want to see him anymore.

"I think I made a mistake," she said slowly, nodding toward a car a row or two over. Most of the people in the parking lot had cleared out already, and Clay spied her car easily. "I don't know why I got so caught up in certain...differences between us. I think we have plenty of time to get to know each other, and I don't think we need to have everything worked out right now."

They arrived at her car, but she didn't get in. "Can you forgive me?"

"Cami." He reached out and tucked her hair behind her ear. "I think it's dangerous that you think I'm so perfect," he said. "For one. But I can forgive you."

"Yeah?" She grinned up at him, a playful glint in her eyes the orange street lamps accentuated.

"Yeah." He swept one arm around her and pulled her into an embrace. She smelled like flowers and mint, and Clay took a deep breath of the scent of her hair. "I sure do like you, and I think if we had enough time, we could fall in love." Clay couldn't believe he'd just said that, but he felt it from head to toe.

"Let's start with the fireside tomorrow night," she said. "We might as well finish out the series, right?"

"Right," Clay said, a ray of sunshine bursting into his life, filling his heart.

"Now, do you really think you can't fit in a sedan?" She giggled, and Clay burst out laughing.

"It's not easy," he admitted. "But I'll try." He started to move around the car, but she grabbed onto his hand.

"Wait a second, cowboy. You're not getting away without giving me a kiss."

"Is that right?" His heartbeat rippled through his chest as she balanced on her toes and touched her mouth to his. Clay cradled her face in his hands and *kissed* her like a man falling in love—because he was.

A COUPLE OF DAYS LATER, CLAY STOOD WITH THE REST OF the congregation at the end of the last fall fireside. The whole series had been fantastic, and while Clay didn't have all the answers to all the questions in the world, he felt satisfied. He knew who he was, and what he wanted, and now he just had to work to get it.

He sang in a loud, clear voice, and when he looked at Cami, she was once again mouthing the words. He smiled and shook his head, but she didn't start singing. The service ended, and she sighed.

"Well," she said, looking up at Clay. "We made it."

"Didn't miss any," he said, smiling down at her. "And now we're having dessert at your grandparents' house, right?"

"It'll be a zoo," Cami said. "I think Granny invited the whole town."

"So we're not going?"

"Oh, we're going," she said. "I'm just warning you."

"I think I can handle it," he said, though he wasn't a fan of crowds. He was a fan of being with Cami, and she had a special relationship with her grandparents.

When Clay pulled up to the cabins along the entrance road at the ranch, there were indeed several cars and trucks parked anywhere possible. A blip of anxiety pulled through him, but he laced his fingers through Cami's and went with her into the cabin.

A zoo was a pretty accurate way to describe the happenings inside the cabin. The scent of chocolate hung in the air, though, and that was enough to keep Clay in the house. People talked, and laughed, and ate brownies and ice cream. Clay simply looked around, taking in the sense of family in the scene before him.

And he loved this family, and he'd count himself lucky to be part of it.

"Hello, Clay," Granny said, and he startled. He wasn't even aware the woman knew his name. "How did you like the firesides?"

"They were amazing," he said. "What about you?"

She shot a glance at Cami. "Oh, that Pastor Dahl. He sometimes says things that make me think too hard."

Clay knew exactly what she was talking about. Cami made a noise Clay didn't know how to classify, and he found her trying to hold back laughter.

He was glad she could laugh about it now, but it sure hadn't been funny on Wednesday night. She let the laughter out, and Clay chuckled with her.

"I'm right," Granny said. "Just like I always make the right match for my grandchildren." She gave them both a knowing look and motioned for them to come get some desserts.

"Is she serious?" Clay asked.

Cami simply smiled and said, "Quite," before leading him over to the brownies.

CHAPTER FIFTEEN

*C*ami stepped over to her sister, her chest pinching. She'd already watched two of her sisters walk down the aisle, pack their lives, and move out of the homestead.

But Jessie's departure felt like it might break Cami. Tonight, she'd sleep in the basement by herself. Rhodes and Capri didn't get married for three more months, and Cami wasn't sure she could survive on her own in that huge house by herself for that long.

"You look so beautiful," she said, her voice cracked so all the emotion came right out.

"Don't cry, Cami," Jessie said, though she was definitely teary herself.

"I can't help it." She drew Jessie into a hug. "We've always been close, and I can't—I mean, I'm so happy for you and Flynn. I'm just...." She shook her head and stepped back, pulling in a breath to steady herself. But she felt anything but steady and strong.

"You're not alone," Jessie said. "I know what you're thinking."

"I can't live in that house by myself."

"Then move into the cabin," Jessie said. "Rhodes has told you that a hundred times."

"I might," Cami said, though she hadn't really considered moving down the road and becoming her brother's next-door neighbor.

"And besides, you and Clay will be married soon enough."

"We're not even engaged," Cami said, brushing Jessie's hand away from her hair. "Leave it. It's perfect."

Jessie faced her, and Cami saw her raw nerves right there in her face. "I'm so nervous. Why am I so nervous?"

"I don't know. It's Flynn, and he's mad for you."

Jessie nodded in short, little bursts of her head. "I'm ready."

"You're ready," Cami said, smiling. She would not ruin her sister's day with her own emotions. "I'll go tell Mom." She embraced her sister one last time and headed out.

She found her parents and told them Jessie was ready, and her dad said, "I'll go get her. You guys go sit down."

Cami linked arms with her mother, who asked, "Am I planning a fifth wedding in the near future?"

"I don't think so, Mom. Clay and I are taking things pretty slowly."

"You sound okay with that."

"I am," Cami said, warmth spreading through her. "I really am."

"Okay, well, go find your boyfriend. Granny's got our seats saved." They went into the banquet hall where the wedding would take place, and Cami slipped onto the end of the row, into a chair beside Clay.

"Hey," she whispered. He immediately lifted his arm around her shoulders and drew her into his body.

"How's she doing?"

"She's ready." She glanced up to the altar, where Flynn stood in his black tuxedo and a dark, dark cowboy hat.

"Will you wear a cowboy hat at our wedding?" she asked Clay.

"Oh, I'm sure I will," he said easily. They'd talked about getting married a few times now, and he never acted like he wasn't going to become her husband eventually. She wasn't impatient for it to happen, but maybe she'd like a clue as to when....

"I'd like that," she said. "My sexy cowboy husband." She snuggled into his side, and he leaned down.

"How are you doing?"

"I'm, uh, okay," she said. "Tonight will be very hard."

"You should stay at the hotel tonight," he said, something he'd suggested before.

"I'm going to have to stay in the homestead alone at some point," she said. "My parents are right there. I'll be okay." She hoped.

"I'll stay late," he said. "And come see you first thing in the morning."

"Really?" she asked, looking up at him.

"Of course." He touched his lips to hers, his cowboy hat bumping against her forehead. The wedding march began, and Cami sat up straighter as she twisted to watch her sister walk down the aisle with their father.

Jessie glowed as if someone had filled her with light bulbs and flipped a switch. She stepped deliberately until their father passed her to Flynn, who likewise looked like the happiest man on earth.

He pressed his cheek to Jessie's, and they faced the pastor together.

Together.

Cami wanted to live her life *together* with someone. With Clay.

❄

WHEN CAMI WOKE THE NEXT MORNING, SHE FELT LIKE she'd been run over by a truck. The wedding, dinner, dance, and reception had taken everything from her. She'd been fairly involved in all the planning and behind-the-scenes for Jessie's wedding, and her mother had been so grateful.

Clay had stayed late, as he'd promised, and Cami found him sitting on the couch in the living room too, the scent of coffee filling the kitchen.

"Morning, beautiful," he said, not bothering to get up. "Coffee's ready, and I brought over that yogurt you like. It's in the fridge."

"Thanks." Cami bypassed the kitchen and came over to him, leaning over the back of the couch as she ran her hand down his chest. She gave him a squeeze, her feelings for him multiplying.

She'd never said those three important words to him, but she found them filling her mouth. "Clay," she said. "I love you."

He sucked in a breath and tilted his head to look at her. Surprise danced in his eyes, and he said, "I love you, too, Cami."

Joy burst through her, and she kissed him as she laughed. "Okay, coffee," she said, skipping away from him.

She opened the cupboard to get down a mug, the motion easy and already underway when she spied something shiny and glinting on the shelf.

A diamond ring.

The mug she'd grabbed fell, clattering and cracking against the countertop. Shock spread through her, and she stumbled backward a step.

Clay appeared at her side, the warmth of his body behind her comforting and strong. "Oh, you found the ring," he said, his voice a little bit too high. He collected the box from the shelf and looked at it.

Then her. "I'm in love with you, Cami Quinn. I know we both want to stay right here on this ranch. I know every fleck of light in your eyes. Every number that you worry about. Every trick you want to teach Trooper."

She pulled in a breath as her emotions threatened to choke her. Clay smiled, the silence between them lengthening as he struggled to contain himself. His emotion touched Cami, and she started crying.

"Will you marry me?" Clay asked, his voice tight.

"Yes," she said, almost before he'd finished asked. "Yes, I'll marry you."

He swept her into his arms, and she hugged him tight, tight, tight. "I love you." He slid the ring on her finger, and she admired it, in total disbelief that she was now engaged.

She looked up at him, some of that glow she'd seen at the wedding yesterday flowing between her and Clay. "And I love you, cowboy."

Read on for a sneak peek at **TEX**, which takes you to Coral Canyon for more amazing cowboy romance! You'll meet the Young family and see old favorites in the Hammonds and Whittakers!

And keep reading to get the coveted Quinn family recipe for Granny's Peach Delight!

GRANNY'S PEACH DELIGHT

Granny's Peach Delight

**NGREDIENTS**

Vanilla wafers

1 stick butter

2 eggs

1 lb. powdered sugar

1 1/2 t. vanilla

4 c. fresh peaches, skinned and sliced

1 c. whipped cream

DIRECTIONS:

1. Layer vanilla wafers in the bottom of a 9x9 baking dish.

2. Mix butter, eggs, powdered sugar and vanilla until well combined.

3. Drop the butter mixture onto wafers and spread to edges of pan.

4. Layer peach slices over butter mixture.

5. Top with whipped cream.

6. Sprinkle 2 crushed vanilla wafers on top.

*T*ex Young drove past the sign welcoming him to Coral Canyon about the same time he realized another song hadn't come up on the radio. He glanced over to his son, who reminded him more of a man than a teenager.

Bryce was seventeen now, with only one more year of high school before he'd be unleashed on the world as an adult. His son met his eye and hastily reached for his phone. "Sorry. I was thinking about something."

Tex thought it was probably some*one*, but he didn't say anything. He didn't quite know how, and living in a permanent place wasn't going to be the only brand new thing Tex would have to learn how to do this summer.

He'd always had Bryce with him in the summers, and he'd loved taking his son around to various cities in the US as he traveled with Country Quad, the family band he'd founded and headed for the past fifteen years.

He smiled at his son and said, "Maybe something that isn't country."

"Are you insane?" Bryce asked with a chuckle. "There is no music other than country that's worth listening to." The twangs of guitar came through the speakers, and Tex did love a good guitar. He'd been playing since he was four years old, and he never felt quite as at-home as he did on a front porch with an instrument in his hands.

Even better was when Bryce sat next to him and sang the songs Tex had written over the years. Otis, one of his brothers in the band, wrote a lot of music and lyrics for the family band, and Tex admired his brother's gift.

Tex shifted in his seat, a question on his mind. He reached to turn down the radio, which also drew Bryce's attention. "You sure you want to stay here for senior year?" he asked.

Bryce looked away, out his passenger window. The boy had been growing facial hair for over a year, and he hadn't shaved since the last day of school, over a week now. Tex had landed in Boise to pick up his son, and they'd spent a handful of days there getting everything packed and loaded into the truck or the trailer currently attached to the hitch behind them.

"Yeah, Dad," he said.

"You never have told me why," Tex said as gently as he could. "Your mother's had you for years."

"Only because you traveled so much," Bryce said. "I came over to your place on every break when you were home."

"Yeah." Tex had traveled three hundred days a year, and while he maintained a residence in Boise, he'd sold that house and rented one in Coral Canyon, Wyoming. He glanced around at the town, noting all the changes. "Wow, look at this medical center."

He'd brought Bryce to his hometown before, when his father had announced he was going to sell the family ranch. Tex had seven brothers, but none of them had felt a deep love for Wyoming land, and no one had wanted the ranch a decade ago, Tex included.

They'd all converged to help Daddy pack, clean, and move

out of the farmhouse and into a more sensible place in the middle of town. He lived with men and women his own age now, without any yardwork, animals to be fed three times a day, or howling winds and snowstorms to navigate to the barn.

Tex actually missed the cowboy life, and he wanted to get back to it. The house he'd rented sat on the other side of town from the ranch where he'd grown up, and he suddenly decided to drive by the farmhouse he'd known so well.

"How are you feeling? Need to use the bathroom? Can we drive by the farmhouse?"

"Sure," Bryce said. "I'm good."

Tex watched the new developments pass by the window, and he saw several new restaurants along this extension of Main Street. "Looks like some great new places to eat," he said.

"Let's try 'em all," Bryce said, referring to a summer he and Tex had spent together a few years ago, where they'd tried as many new restaurants as they could, in as many towns and cities as possible.

"Deal," Tex said with a smile. He passed the road that led back to the high school, then City Hall, then the library. Tex couldn't remember the last book he'd read, and he wondered if he should make a list of things he wanted to try this summer.

Reading would go on it. *Getting back to his cowboy roots* would too. *Writing a new song, getting and riding a new horse*, and *hiking* would definitely be on it.

"Maybe we should make a summer list," he said, glancing over to his son. "Things we haven't done it a while we want to do, or things around Coral Canyon we can't do anywhere else."

"Like the balloon festival,"

"Yeah," Tex said, grinning. "Like that."

"I heard there's a police dog academy here," Bryce said. "And they do tours."

"We'll look it up when we get to the house." Tex made another turn, and the road led past a couple of office buildings and then the residential part of Coral Canyon opened up. The houses along these streets sat fairly close together, and the farther they got from the historic Main Street, the more land surrounded the houses.

"Did you like growing up out here?" Bryce asked.

"Yeah," Tex said, sighing. "We had a pond right on the property. We could ride our bikes anywhere. Dad let us go fishing every Sunday after church." He grinned at his son. "It was an easy, slow life."

He had liked it, and the tender part of his heart longed for that life again. He'd stepped back from Country Quad to do exactly that, hadn't he? Relax more. Travel less. Find a community to belong to?

He had, and his chest swelled with another breath, which he blew out slowly. "It was a good life." He looked at his son again. "What happened in Boise to make you want to leave everything you've known and come do your senior year here?"

His dad had always shot straight with him, and Tex wasn't doing his son any favors by not making him talk. He'd stayed in touch with his son over the years, but Tex wouldn't label himself a good father.

He could talk to his son, and he'd given his advice over the years, but he hadn't been involved in the day-to-day parenting the way his ex-wife had. He knew that had been a major source of annoyance to Corrie, the woman he'd been married to for only two years before that marriage had dissolved.

He was actually looking forward to this summer and this year and all of this time off. He would finally be able to dedicate time and energy to Bryce, and they'd talked about this year a lot already on the drive here from Boise.

"Mom's...she's been saying some things."

Tex kept his gaze out the windshield. "What kind of things?"

"Lots of stuff," he said. "When she said she had put her whole life on hold to have me and she couldn't wait to do what she wanted, I got pretty mad at her. There was...sort of a...blow up."

Tex didn't know what to say. His chest stormed and his stomach turned inside out. "She loves you," he said.

"She told me she hated being a mom," Bryce said. "That's when I called you."

Tex whipped his attention to Bryce. "She did not say that."

"She said she wished she'd never had kids." Bryce kept his gaze out the window. "It's fine. I don't believe her, and I know she's been stressed."

"About what?" Tex demanded, trying to keep his grip on the steering wheel loose. "All the money I send her for the two of you? Her summers off from teaching? That perfect, two-story house that looks like it came out of a storybook?"

Bryce said nothing, and Tex stewed in his anger. Corrie had no right to make Bryce feel like he was unwanted.

"Bud," he said. "I'm sorry. I know she didn't mean any of those things."

"Yeah, I know too," he said. "But since you were coming already, and we always have the summers, I just figured, why not senior year too?"

"Jenny's why-not-senior-year-too," Tex said, sliding his man-son a look out of the corner of his eye. "You're still talking to her, right?"

"Yeah," Bryce said with a sigh. "We talk."

"You goin' with her?"

"I don't know what that means, Dad," he teased.

"It means she's your girlfriend." Tex gave him a full look.

"Your mother told me about the Sweethearts dance and the prom, and then the other prom...."

"Yeah, well, she lives in Boise, and I live here now."

Tex made another turn, this time not looking at his son. "Once we have a real chance, we'll look around and buy something. I'm going to stay here for a while." The right side of the road didn't have any houses, and the places out here were spaced far apart.

"Whenever," Bryce said. "We can put it on our summer list."

"I used to go with the girl who lived next door to me," Tex said, infusing a smile into his voice.

"You've told me, Dad," Bryce said dryly.

"See? You know what goin' with someone means."

Bryce scoffed—or maybe laughed—and shook his head. "All right, Pops."

Tex laughed too, saying, "It's right up here."

"You sure?" Bryce asked. "I've been here before, and it didn't look like this."

Tex frowned out the window too, because his son was right. The land sat in shades of yellow and brown. The fence that ran around the pasture that bordered the road looked like it could collapse if a two-ounce bird swooped down and landed on it.

"Maybe no one lives here," he mused. He didn't know who his father had sold the ranch to, and it had been ten years anyway. The property could've changed hands more than once by now.

The pasture gave way to the house and lawn, but it too looked abandoned. No one lived here, that was for dang sure.

"Look," Bryce said. "There's a sign. Is the house for sale?"

Tex's heart jumped right up into his throat. If this house and ranch was up for sale, he wanted to buy it. "Is it?" He slowed the truck he'd owned for years and turned into the gravel driveway. Weeds and grass grew through the rocks, along with some pretty pink wildflowers Tex had long forgotten the name of.

He brought the vehicle to a stop long before the end of the driveway, which would take him all the way to the back steps. His mother would throw a fit if she saw the state of the front porch she'd once loved and tended to.

Tex could remember trimming this lawn behind a push mower, and he knew how to fix fences, tend to horses and cattle, and paint houses. His father had made his boys do all of it as they grew up, and he'd pitched in plenty.

He must be so disappointed in us, Tex thought as he looked at the house. Half of the brothers had passed on inheriting the ranch because of the band. The twins were still heavily entrenched in the rodeo and had barely been out of the house when Daddy had decided he was too old and too weak to keep up the two-hundred-acre ranch.

"Dad," Bryce said, and Tex blinked his eyes to get himself to stop looking at the peeling paint and the faded front door. He hadn't even noticed his son getting out of the truck. Bryce stood on the lawn—the crispy, brown grass—and waved at Tex to come over.

He heaved a sigh and got out of the truck, the heat of the day punching him in the lungs. It wasn't usually hot in the mountains, but the whole country was experiencing a heat wave this week.

"What is it?" he asked.

"There's an auction on this property," Bryce said. "Tomorrow."

"Tomorrow?" Tex arrived and looked at the sign, but the type was way too small to hold his attention for long. He'd always had such a short attention span, and he forced himself to read the big, blocky, black letters.

The property would be sold as-is to the highest bidder.

The auction would be at the library at ten a.m. in the morning, and Tex's only thought was that he better be there.

"We should go," Bryce said. "You have some money, right, Dad?"

"A little," Tex said. Enough to buy a house with a loan. This was a cash auction, and Tex wondered how much it would go for. In Coral Canyon, Wyoming? A town of maybe twelve thousand? After a rush of growth? With other houses sitting empty?

"Let's look at the market," Tex said.

"I want to sit on the porch where you kissed Nina," Bryce said, chuckling as he jogged across the grass.

"That was eons ago," Tex called after his son. He returned his attention to his phone, and he started looking up the real estate market in Coral Canyon. The town had enjoyed a boom a few years ago, but the growth had stalled, and Tex didn't see anything out of his price range.

A broken-down, abandoned ranch further from town? No one would want this place, and Tex suddenly did. He could call Otis, Blaze, and Trace and find out if they'd like to go in on the ranch with him.

The band was taking a break this summer, as his brothers were trying to figure out if they wanted to rebrand Country Quad into Country Trio—or some other name—and continue making music, or if anyone else was ready to do something different with his life.

Tex knew Blaze didn't want to keep traveling. He'd been talking to a woman pretty seriously over a dating app, and he'd gone to Florida to meet her. Tex was expecting a text announcing his brother's engagement any moment now.

Otis and Trace had stayed in Nashville for now, but they were taking time off. Tex could text them both about chipping in for the ranch and get them out here to Wyoming by next weekend.

Cash only, streamed through his head. Country Quad had kept their calendar booked, but they weren't mega-stars. And they had to split the money four ways. Tex had always had enough for his needs, to send to Corrie and Bryce, and to enjoy himself without thinking too hard about how he'd pay for his next meal.

"You can't be on this property," a woman said, and Tex looked up from his phone. The sunlight glinted off his front windshield, momentarily blinding him. The woman's voice tickled something familiar inside him, but he couldn't quite place it.

"This is private property," she said. "We don't need any land sharks coming into our town." She marched on toward him, her long legs clad in jeans despite the heat. She also wore a blue and white striped tank top and cowgirl boots on her feet. Her limbs were long, and she ate up the distance between them in a few last strides.

By then, Tex knew exactly who she was. Fireworks popped inside him, burning his lungs and rendering his voice mute.

Abigail Ingalls put one hand on her hip and gestured toward the porch. "Do you mind getting him off the porch?"

"Sure," Tex said, the word catching in his throat. He whistled through his teeth, something he'd always done to call his son and get him to come back to him. He'd been doing it since the boy could crawl, and it worked now too. Tex could barely look away from Abby, but in the brief moment he did, he saw Bryce coming down the steps and toward him.

"Sorry, Abby," he said, reaching up to tip his cowboy hat at her. He was suddenly so glad he'd bought it, because it hid his lack of hair, something he'd become more and more self-conscious about in the past couple of years.

The woman folded her arms now. "Do I know you?"

Bryce jogged up, and Tex indicated the truck. "We should go."

"Yeah, sure," he said, but he simply looked at Tex and then Abby. Abby looked back and forth between the two of them, her gaze finally landing on Tex, her eyebrows cocked high as she obviously waited for him to explain.

"You should know me," he said. "I took you to plenty of drive-in movies. A dance or two. I think I even told my son here about how I used to duck into your barn so we could sneak a kiss." He grinned at Abby, but a horrified expression filled her face instead of the fun, flirty vibe Tex had been trying for.

Ooh, more cowboys in Coral Canyon, and this land war is going to put hearts on the line... **You can read <u>TEX</u>, the first book in the Coral Canyon Cowboys series, right now in paperback!**

Contracted Cowboy (Book 1): A fake ad brings a cowboy to Georgia's door just in time for all the Quinn family holiday parties, so she hires Logan to be her boyfriend. Nothing can go wrong with this plan...except she might lose her heart to her newly contracted cowboy.

Secret Sweetheart (Book 2): She's a domestic goddess. He works on her father's ranch. They could have forever...if they could take their relationship out of the shadows. **Can she overcome her anxiety and fear and build a life with Knox? Or will their relationship be doomed to die in the shadows at Quinn Valley Ranch?**

Landscaping Love (Book 3): He hired her to landscape the yard, but she's going to make him re-evaluate who he lets into his heart. **Can Rhodes and Capri landscape their love? Or will they go their separate ways once the yard is finished?**

Birthday Boyfriend (Book 4): This Quinn cowgirl doesn't need a lot for her birthday...just the cowboy she's been crushing on for months. Will Flynn ever see Jessie standing right in front of him?

Fall Fireside (Book 5): Cami Quinn has had enough of being the shiny new date for the cowboys in Quinn Valley. She's on her fifth or sixth broken heart, and she needs the soothing, healing messages she's found at the fall fireside series in the past. Will Cami and Clay find a way to mend what's broken inside themselves in order to find a happily-ever-after?

BOOKS IN THE CORAL CANYON COWBOYS ROMANCE SERIES

Tex (Book 1): He's back in town after a successful country music career. She owns a bordering farm to the family land he wants to buy...and she outbids him at the auction. Can Tex and Abigail rekindle their old flame, or will the issue of land ownership come between them?

Otis (Book 2): He's finished with his last album and looking for a soft place to fall after a devastating break-up. She runs the small town bookshop in Coral Canyon and needs a new boyfriend to get her old one out of her life for good. Can Georgia convince Otis to take another shot at real love when their first kiss was fake?

Morris (Book 3): Morris Young is just settling into his new life as the manager of Country Quad when he attends a wedding. He sees his ex-wife there—apparently Leighann is back in Coral Canyon—along with a little boy who can't be more or less than five years old... Could he be Morris's? And why is his heart hoping for that, and for a reconciliation with the woman who left him because he traveled too much?

Trace (Book 4): He's been accused of only dating celebrities. She's a simple line dance instructor in small town Coral Canyon, with a soft spot for kids...and cowboys. Trace could use some dance lessons to go along with his love lessons... Can he and Everly fall in love with the beat, or will she dance her way right out of his arms?

Blaze (Book 5): He's dark as night, a single dad, and a retired bull riding champion. With all his money, his rugged good looks, and his ability to say all the right things, Faith has no chance against Blaze Young's charms. But she's his complete opposite, and she just doesn't see how they can be together...

...so she ends things with him.

Gabe (Book 6): He's a father's rights advocate lawyer with a sweet little girl. She's fighting for her own daughter. Can Gabe and Hilde find happily-ever-after when they're at such odds with one another?

Jem (Book 7): He's still healing from his vices, and Jem has dedicated everything he has to his two kids. At least he's not mourning his divorce anymore, and in fact, he might be ready to move on. She's his former best friend, and once he breaks his wrist, his nurse. Can Sunny somehow rope this cowboy's heart?

Luke (Book 7): He swore off women when his ex told him he might not be their daughter's father. But a paternity test confirmed he is, and Luke Young has dedicated his life to his little girl and his brothers' band. There hasn't been time for a girlfriend anyway. He's tried here and there, and the women in small-town Coral Canyon are certainly interested in him.

ABOUT LIZ

Liz Isaacson writes inspirational romance, usually set in Texas, or Wyoming, or anywhere else horses and cowboys exist. She lives in Utah, where she writes full-time, takes her two dogs to the park everyday, and eats a lot of veggies while writing. Find her on her website at feelgoodfictionbooks.com